"It's our

He clasped her hand in his, giving her fingers a reassuring squeeze. "And you and our baby *could never* be a burden to me."

She stepped back, her fingers tingling, her insides feeling like they were ready to combust into flames of desire. And all from just one brief touch. What would happen if they got a heck of a lot closer emotionally, too?

She did not want to get involved with someone who could not—did not—love her. Not again.

"I promise I will always be here for the two of you," he continued huskily.

She paused an uncomfortable length of time. She went over to look out the front windows to check on the progress of the approaching storm, which seemed to be getting closer. "You say that now..."

He followed her, stood looking out at the thick gray clouds dominating the horizon. Then turned to her. "I mean it now."

They were close enough, she could feel the body heat emanating from his tall, strong frame. "You think you do."

Dear Reader,

Christmas is the season of unexpected miracles. Gift giving and receiving. Making impossible wishes and having them magically come true. And putting our hope and faith in the days and nights to come.

Freedom-loving Travis Lockhart, however, doesn't have anything in particular on his wish list. The part-time cowboy and full-time handyman has plenty of family in Laramie County to spend the yuletide with. He's content helping clients make *their* holiday dreams come true, while keeping his own commitments and possessions to a minimum.

Twice-orphaned Skye McPherson yearns to have a family of her own again...and a permanent home to go to. She's given up on it ever happening until a sudden inheritance, tied to an arranged marriage, is presented to her and Travis. All they have to do is enter into a hundred-and-twenty-day marriage, and the Winding Creek ranch will be theirs!

Skye sees this as a chance of a lifetime and wants to go for it. Travis says, "Not so fast." Marriage was serious business, even one in name only.

Had it not been for their love of the couple who willed the property to them, they might have remained in a stalemate. But they did want to honor Walter and Willa Braeloch's crazlly romantic last wishes.

So Skye and Travis said "I do" and enter into a Christmas season neither would ever forget!

I hope you have a wonderful holiday with your loved ones, and that all your yuletide dreams come true!

Cathy Gillen Thacker

Their Texas
Christmas Match

—

CATHY GILLEN THACKER

HARLEQUIN
SPECIAL
EDITION

HARLEQUIN®
SPECIAL EDITION™

Recycling programs
for this product may
not exist in your area.

ISBN-13: 978-1-335-72433-5

Their Texas Christmas Match

Copyright © 2022 by Cathy Gillen Thacker

For questions and comments about the quality of this book,
please contact us at CustomerService@Harlequin.com.

Harlequin Enterprises ULC
22 Adelaide St. West, 41st Floor
Toronto, Ontario M5H 4E3, Canada
www.Harlequin.com

Printed in U.S.A.

Cathy Gillen Thacker is a married mother of three. She and her husband reside in North Carolina. Her stories have made numerous appearances on bestseller lists, but her best reward is knowing one of her books made someone's day a little brighter. A popular Harlequin author, she loves telling passionate stories with happy endings and thinks nothing beats a good romance and a hot cup of tea! Visit her at cathygillenthacker.com for information on her books, recipes and a list of her favorite things.

Chapter One

"We're talking about an *arranged* marriage," Travis Lockhart said gruffly. He stared at Skye McPherson, barely able to believe she would even entertain such a crazy notion. A lively spark appeared in the stunning brunette's dark brown eyes. To his consternation, she seemed as unaffected by the unconventional terms of Willa and Walter Braeloch's bequest as he was utterly dumbfounded.

"Oh, I'm aware, cowboy," she drawled right back.

The late-afternoon sun bathed the front porch of the Winding Creek ranch house, catching the golden blond highlights that framed her face, providing what little warmth there was on that mid-November day in Laramie, Texas. She had suggested they take this meeting outside, and he and the attorney delivering the news had readily agreed. They all wanted the will-reading over with as quickly as possible.

Like Travis, Skye was unable to sit still. "But it's not as if it has to be a *real* marriage." She straightened her slender shoulders, drawing herself up to her full five-foot-eight-inch height. Still in her nurse's scrubs, her hair drawn into a sophisticated knot on the back of her head, she turned to Travis's brother-in-law, Griffith Montgomery, who had drawn up the late couple's unconventional wills. He was sitting in one of the cushioned chairs on the covered front porch, briefcase opened on the table next to him.

Skye peered at Griff expectantly, then stopped pacing and sat down next to the lawyer. "Does it?"

He cleared his throat and looked distinctly uncomfortable. "That is correct. There's nothing in the terms that says your union must be consummated…"

She turned back to Travis with a triumphant smile. "See?"

"But," the attorney continued, "there is a provision that says no annulment will be possible if you want to inherit. At the end of the 120-day marriage, you will either have to continue your relationship as husband and wife or divorce."

Still feeling a little shell-shocked, Travis lounged against one of the pillars that supported the one-story porch extending all the way across the front of the three-story Victorian and down one side. "And if we decide not to marry at all, then what?"

"The same thing that happens if you get hitched

and then split up before the 120 days are up," Griff explained. "The property will be sold to the highest bidder, which in this case is a custom home builder who will turn the Winding Creek's two thousand acres into a luxury-home subdivision. The profits from the sale will then be put in a general welfare trust, paid out for both of you, only as needed, for a maximum of fifty thousand per person, per year."

Travis and Skye both took a moment to absorb all that. Already not liking the way this was shaking out, he asked casually, "Who administers the trust?"

"Joe Carson, one of the founding members of my law firm," Griff replied.

Travis studied his sister Mackenzie's husband, whose own convenient marriage had, against all odds, turned into an epic love story. "I'm guessing this boss of yours is a stickler for the rules?"

"You better believe it."

Sighing, he squinted at the gloomy clouds building up along the horizon, theorizing. "If the property has sold and the money's in trust, and I wanted a new truck for my business…"

Griff saw where this was going. "Joe Carson'd probably consider it." He leaned forward, warning, "But if you wanted a fancy sports car when you already have a vehicle that runs just fine, he probably would not. Because that item would not be considered necessary for your general welfare."

Clearly weary of this conversation, Skye stood and began to pace once again, her long legs moving effortlessly and slender hips swaying gently beneath the black cotton scrub pants. "That's all fine with me," she interrupted, making her own feelings clear. "I wouldn't want to spend any of the money we inherited, anyway. I'd just feel safer knowing it was there, in case of an emergency…"

Travis's gaze clashed with Skye's. It was easy to see she still thought the worst of him—assuming she thought about him at all. She likely didn't. Whereas he dreamed about her nearly every night since they'd recklessly hooked up out of grief over Walter's and Willa's deaths.

Noting the way the breeze plastered her sweater against her delectable breasts, he turned his gaze back to her face. "That's not really the point," he said, ignoring the hardening of his body.

Griff interjected, working to get them back on track, "Actually, having an executor or administrator in charge is precisely the point of a general welfare trust."

Travis blew out a frustrated breath. "It's someone else having control over any part of my life that I don't like."

"So you're saying, what?" Skye countered, completely misreading him, as usual. "If you *were* to inherit a million dollars, you'd run right out and spend it all?"

He met her testy glare with one of his own. "No. I'd probably just put it in the bank or a very safe investment like more land. But *I'd* get to decide. *I* wouldn't be relying on anyone else to agree with my decision of what to do."

She propped her hands on her hips, squinting right

back at him. "Well, with that attitude, you're going to be a very difficult beneficiary."

Maybe. Or maybe not, since he didn't really intend to touch the money, whether it was legally his or not.

"Not to mention," she continued emotionally, "a very difficult husband."

Travis agreed. He wasn't cut out for marriage. Not at all. Which was exactly why this bequest was such a bad idea. Not that it could be changed now.

He just wished Walter and Willa hadn't played matchmaker…

Skye seemed surprised that he hadn't responded to her insult. She trod closer, inundating him with her sunny citrus scent. "What? You got *nothing*?" she challenged, planting her sneaker-clad feet on the wooden porch floor.

Remembering this very spot was where they had first kissed, he pushed away the renewed burst of desire and rolled his eyes at her deliberately haughty tone. "Only because I agree with you, darlin'. I would indeed make a lousy spouse. Which is exactly why I'm the only one of my siblings who has never gotten hitched." Although once, he had foolishly come close…only to have his heart stomped all to pieces.

Griff impatiently glanced at his watch. "As amusing as all this repartee is, can we get back to the situation at hand?"

"Gladly," Travis said, eager to get this over with so he could get back to his solo life. "So, if we want full control of the money—"

Griff laid it out flatly: "You have to follow the terms of the will and embark on a 120-day marriage."

Skye bit her lip, for the first time seeming to consider another option than the one just set out for them by Willa and Walter's attorney. "And if we were to accept the developer's bid as is, without marrying. What would happen to the ranch house?"

Where she currently lived.

"And the dogtrot cabin?" she continued. *Where he lived.*

"And the barn where I currently house the workshop for my handyman business," Travis jumped in. He had assumed—wrongly, it appeared—that he and Skye would be able to carve out the ten acres or so of land around the buildings and remain in the residences they'd called home for the last couple of years.

Griff grimaced. "The developer's clear. He'll tear everything down. Nothing of the Winding Creek Ranch will be left. But if the two of you want to eventually live on one of the ten-acre estates in one of his luxury custom-built homes, he said he will give you first pick of the lots."

Travis waved off the offer. "Not interested," he said, knowing the subdivision life was not for him.

He needed wide-open spaces. Beautiful sunsets and sunrises. The peace and quiet only country life could bring.

Skye pressed her soft lips together. "Me either." She turned to look Travis in the eye, her protective attitude toward the late couple clear. "Because there is no way that I am going to consent to a sale or let Willa and Walter's entire life's legacy be torn down."

I may as well have announced my intention to have an alien baby, Skye thought as the two men stared at her skeptically.

"I don't see that we have any other choice but to sell," Travis said finally.

"Sure, we do," Skye pressed on. "We could get married for four months. Just like Willa and Walter stipulated. And use that time to figure out how to keep their ranch going in the way they envisioned—with a happy family living here."

He scoffed. "Yeah, well, that definitely won't be us," he countered in a low, gravelly tone that brought back unwanted sensual memories, electrifying every nerve in her body.

"No joke, Sherlock," Skye retorted, frustrated that once again, Travis Lockhart had jumped to the wrong conclusion about her. Which wasn't all that uncommon. He had spent the initial two years they had lived on the ranch steadfastly going the other way and avoiding interaction with her.

Except for the night of the joint memorial for the ninety-year-old couple, who had passed within days of each other. When she and Travis had both opened up their hearts and let their guards down, to disastrous results...

Ever since, they had gone back to the safety of avoiding each other as much as humanly possible. Keeping their communication to texting and email only. Limiting even that to business matters of the ranch, most of which were currently being handled by the Fort Worth law firm where Griff worked.

She forced herself to go back to the unusual bequest. "But I feel sure, if we highlight all the improvements Willa and Walter had us start two years ago and turn the marketing of the property over to a high-end Realtor from Dallas or Houston, that they would be able to find a very wealthy family, with kids, looking for a country spread, who could outbid the developer."

Travis paused. He ran his hand through his thick and rumpled walnut-brown hair. Cut short and casual, it seemed to go every which way in a style she found completely natural and unbearably sexy. He, too, had come straight from work, knocking off a bit early, just as she had. Travis was dressed in worn jeans and a plaid flannel shirt that made the most of the taut abs, muscular chest and broad shoulders on his six-foot-two-inch frame. His boots were scuffed, his square jaw clean-shaven. Lips masculine and as perfect in that rough-hewn way as the rest of him. But it was his kind yet perceptive whiskey-colored eyes that turned her on the most.

But her attraction to him only went so far. His determination to live life solo, and go his own way in his own time, was a total turnoff.

Which was kind of ironic, given she had decided on the same path for herself.

One broken heart had been enough.

Picking up the threads of her argument, she met his considering glance and continued lobbying for what she knew was best. "And then the Winding Creek Ranch would be the lively family home Willa and Walter always envisioned it being one day."

Exhaling, Travis folded his arms. "That's a good point," he said quietly. "Walter and Willa always dreamed of having children living here. Especially since they were never able to have any kids of their own. The Braeloch line ended with the two of them. And they wanted Winding Creek to be passed from one generation to the next."

And family, she knew, was Travis's one weak spot. Just as it was hers. In different ways, of course.

He was one of eight tragically orphaned kids who had been adopted by Robert and Carol Lockhart. Whereas she was an only child, who had been raised by her great-aunt after her parents perished in a freak accident when she was very young. When she was sixteen, her aunt had died, turning her life upside down once again.

So unlike the taciturn cowboy in front of her, who had more family than he could count, she was still all alone in the world.

And, she was beginning to think, probably always would be. But that wouldn't stop her from doing what was right.

Travis looked at Skye for a long moment, then turned back to Griff, who was still sitting in one of the Adirondack chairs, legal papers strewn out in front of him. "Are you sure there is no other way to preserve the Winding Creek as a family ranch?"

"Willa and Walter were quite clear in what they wanted."

Travis sighed, exactly the way she had months ago, when the outlandish idea had first been floated as a possibility. Not that she had ever imagined the hopelessly romantic couple would actually go through with rewriting their last wills and testaments...

He frowned, continuing, "And what they wanted was for Skye and me to give marriage a try."

Griff nodded.

"How long do we have to decide?" she asked.

Griff stood and handed them both their copies of the wills. "As long as you need. But I would advise you to make a decision quickly so that the will can be filed with the court and go through probate. In the meantime—" he handed them a thumb drive "—Willa and Walter recorded a message for the two of you to watch together."

After Griff left, Travis turned to Skye. "Your place or mine?" he joked wryly.

She gave him a look that let him know clowning around was not welcome. Unfortunately, lame jokes were what got him through the toughest moments in life. So he cocked a brow and waited.

"I won't put the moves on you again, if that's what you're worried about," he said.

She rolled her eyes at him, deftly avoiding any further talk about their Big Mistake—the night of the dual memorial services, nearly three months ago—or the frigid silence that had existed between them ever since. "Believe me, I'm not the least bit worried about that."

"Good. Because one wrong turn was enough, as far as I'm concerned," he couldn't resist adding.

She nodded stiffly. "For both of us." Then she turned on her heel and led the way into the ranch house. Most of it had been updated and refreshed over the last few years. While she had been living there as the Braelochs' private duty nurse slash companion, he had served as the ranch caretaker in addition to his full-time work as a handyman. Hence, the two had been so busy, they rarely even crossed paths, which suited them both.

She walked through the high-ceilinged hallway, past the sweeping staircase and formal living and dining rooms, to the rear of the home, where a large country kitchen, mudroom and small sitting room were located.

Her laptop was open on the kitchen table.

After sitting down and powering it on, she motioned for him to take a chair, too.

He grabbed a kitchen chair, turned it around backward and straddled it. Arms folded across the padded back, he watched as she plugged in the thumb drive and opened up the file.

Walter and Willa Braeloch appeared on-screen. They were sitting in this very kitchen, their chairs pulled together.

Willa was wearing one of the denim ranch dresses she favored. Her short, curly white hair was freshly permed; her soft cheeks were rosy; and her faded blue eyes beamed with a mix of determination and excitement.

Walter was wearing a denim shirt open at the throat. His full silver hair was neatly combed, his face cleanly shaven. The old man's gray eyes were serious yet somehow loving and accepting.

At ninety, each had suffered health challenges but managed to live life fully just the same. Travis had never been able to do anything but admire them.

"Well…" Willa reached over and took Walter's hand. "Skye and Travis… I guess if you two are watching this, it means we have moved on to our next great adventure. Which means the Winding Creek Ranch is in need of new stewardship. Our attorney, Griff Montgomery, told you of our request that our beloved ranch pass permanently to the two of you. But only if you two are married and plan a future here. Hopefully, one with the children we were never able to have."

"It probably sounds like a crazy bequest," her husband cut in. "But Willa and I have seen the sparks between the two of you. We know how much you have in common. And we truly believe that, given the chance, you could bring out the absolute best in each other the way Willa and I have."

Willa added, "We know how much Skye loves living in the country—and the life Travis could bring to this property."

"Which is why we have put fifty thousand dollars for interim property management in a trust managed by our law firm. It already has and will continue to pay all the expenses until the property is either sold or reverts permanently to the two of you," Walter said.

"And while we understand all this is probably coming as something of a shock to you two, we also want to remind you that arranged marriages can work out spectacularly," Willa said.

Walter added, "Willa and I—and our happy marriage—can attest to that."

Willa beamed beside him.

"Of course, there are a few stipulations," Walter continued. "The first is that you spend every night beneath the same roof and enjoy at least one meal together every day. Finances are a big part of every marriage, so you have to agree on how any money is spent and the final disposition of the ranch."

Walter and Willa exchanged loving glances; then Willa went on, "Basically, we're asking that you both give your union the honor and due diligence marriage deserves."

"Then, if it still doesn't work out the way *we* think it will," Walter said, giving his wife another confident look before turning back to the camera, "the two of you'll be able to move on, all the wiser and more financially secure for the experience."

"In the meantime," Willa said, suddenly beginning to choke up, "just know that the two of you are the children we never had and always wanted."

"And that we will both always love and treasure our time with you," Walter said in a low rusty-sounding voice.

Willa began to cry in earnest. He took her into his arms. Then the video ended. Eyes filling, Travis turned to Skye. Her eyes were overflowing, too. His heart went out to her, and he did the only thing he knew to do—he reached out and pulled her close. Surprisingly, she did not resist.

Chapter Two

"I don't know why I'm crying," Skye blubbered.

"Probably same reason as me." Travis's gruff voice was muffled against the top of her head. "Losing the Braelochs has been hard as hell on both of us."

He was right about that. Remembering all too well what had happened the last time they allowed themselves to physically console each other for their loss, Skye eased out of his strong arms, then went in search of a tissue box. "Still… I thought I was over the worst of my grief."

He pushed his chair back, stood and waited while she wiped the tears from her face before swinging back to face him. "Me too." He curved his big calloused hands over the edge of the chair. "Today brought it all back."

"You're right about that," Skye responded, wishing

Travis wasn't so damned sensitive to her feelings. She had never met anyone as inherently kind and gallant as he was. The fact that he was Texas-cowboy hot and made love with incredible tenderness and skill made him even harder to resist. But knowing how opposed he felt about getting too emotionally attached to any one person or place required her to do just that.

It's happening again, Travis thought. Skye was running hot and cold on him. Letting him close one minute, pulling away the next.

Hands trembling, she wandered over to the new stainless steel French door refrigerator that was so at odds with most everything else—except the brand-new microwave, four-burner stove and dishwasher—in the big, charmingly outdated country kitchen. She pulled out a pitcher of iced tea and busied herself by filling glasses with ice. "I guess it was something about seeing Willa and Walter on-screen—hearing their voices— that brought it all back."

Travis scrubbed a palm over his face. "Losing them both last August to a late-summer cold was a shock." One day, they'd had the sniffles; the next, Skye was insisting they go to the ER, prevailing on Travis to help transport them.

She added mint leaves to the tall glasses and handed him one, their lightly brushing fingers sending a new tingle of unwanted awareness through him. She met his gaze. "It's not uncommon for elderly patients like Willa and Walter, who both had preexisting conditions, to succumb to even minor illnesses."

They had slipped into comas, one by one, and then passed within hours of each other, with Skye sitting at Willa's bedside and Travis at Walter's. Each holding their hand and doing their best to make it a moment of peace and love.

His lips flattening in renewed grief, Travis breathed in and took a long draught of tea. Skye met his eyes again, her experience as a critical care nurse coming into play. "They talked about wanting to go at the same time."

Travis nodded, the ache in his throat practically strangling him. "I know being together was what they always wanted."

Skye neared, drawing his attention to the classically beautiful features of her face. He inhaled the fragrance unique to her and felt his heartbeat quicken.

She drew in a breath. "Now, we have to talk about what else Walter and Willa wanted."

"The arranged marriage."

Skye nodded, self-conscious color coming into her cheeks.

"It's a crazy idea," he said.

"Not really," she countered, "considering they were brought together by their parents."

"Seventy years ago," he said, irked to have her go all idealistic on him now. "When those kinds of marital arrangements were the norm!"

She looked down her nose at him. "Willa said from what she had seen, young people had not only lost the will to marry but the art of proper courtship as well."

Travis grimaced. "So what are you saying? That the

terms of the will were Willa and Walter's nudge for us to try to find everlasting love?"

"Yes." She ran a hand through her sexy side-swept bangs.

He studied her, realizing she might be more romantic, deep down, than he had ever imagined. Unless she was really in this for the money. In which case, all bets were off.

Unable to resist the chance to openly challenge her, he prodded, "I still don't understand why you would be so willing to get hitched." He gazed at her, long and hard. Marriage was a huge undertaking.

Shooting him an exasperated look, she went to the canvas bag she had taken to work and pulled out a few bento boxes. "I'm not sure I can explain."

"Try." He watched her rinse the lunch containers out in the sink before sliding them into the dishwasher. Because if she couldn't come up with a good reason, there was no way he would even entertain this.

With a huff, she turned back around to face him. "Well, unlike you, I don't have any family."

Abruptly, he realized how little he really knew about her. Except that she was extremely well respected in the medical community as both a rural private duty and critical care nurse. And she didn't seem to date. At least, not that he had seen. "No one?"

She shook her head. "I was born in Amarillo and spent my early years in north Texas. My parents died in a white water rafting accident when I was eight, and my great-aunt Eileen took me in. I lived with her on her vegetable farm in Illinois until I was sixteen. They were happy times."

"Is that why you resurrected Willa's old vegetable garden after you moved in? And started pruning her blackberry bushes and fruit trees?"

"Willa lamented not being able to do it anymore. And I always loved working outside. So it made us both happy."

Travis could see that. The two women had spent a lot of time during the previous two springs sitting outside, deciding what to plant where. Occasionally, there had been a basket of fresh produce left outside his door when he got home at the end of a long workday. "What happened to your great-aunt?"

Skye's face fell. "She died of a stroke. The farm had to be sold, and because there was no other family to take me, I went into foster care. And from there, on to nursing school and eventually a job in Chicago."

"How did you end up in Laramie County?"

She ran a hand over the kitchen cabinets she had painted a sophisticated sage green. Another home-improvement project she'd done with Willa that had had both of them brainstorming and Skye doing all the work while Willa—and sometimes Walter, too—happily kept her company.

"Did the Midwest not suit you?"

Skye evaded his eyes, then admitted after a reluctant sigh, "Let's just say I wasn't happy working and living in the big city anymore, and I wanted to get back to my Texas roots. I saw an ad for a job dealing with homebound patients here and thought it might be the change I needed."

"And that's how you met Willa and Walter."

"Yes. Initially, they just needed me to come by a couple times a week. But eventually, it was either have a caretaker move in full-time or they were going to have to sell and move into a nursing home." Skye shrugged. "So they offered me the gig, and I took it."

"They were lucky to have you."

"And you. If you hadn't been here on the premises to do all the heavy lifting and keep the fields mowed, the fences repaired—life probably would have looked a lot different to them."

His eyes glimmered with emotion. "They treated me like a son."

"And me, like a daughter. I really loved them." Her voice broke.

"Me too," he agreed gruffly.

She laid a hand over her heart. "And I really want to honor them by fulfilling their last request and finding a happy family, complete with children, to live on Winding Creek—just the way the Braelochs always dreamed."

To Skye's surprise, Travis looked more amenable than he had at the start of the conversation. He rubbed the back of his neck. "You'd really be okay with a marriage of convenience?"

Now that he'd said it out loud, it made her feel…odd. Like she was resigning herself to being one of those people who never enjoyed a bigger-than-life romance but instead were always stuck in mediocrity. Doing her best to hide her feelings, she deadpanned, "That's not a term you hear much these days."

Her joke fell flat.

"You know what I mean," Travis gritted out.

Unfortunately, she did. "Yes, I am adult enough to be able to handle living under one roof together, for however long it takes to realize Walter and Willa's dreams for their property."

"You're not concerned about what people will say?" he asked.

"That I'm a gold digger who would do anything for money?"

He braced his hands on his waist and sized her up with a glance. "That we're *both* opportunists who would do anything for a buck. Even enter into an arranged marriage."

Without warning, Skye's heart began to pound. "I guess there's no way we can reasonably expect to keep this part of the deal quiet."

Inscrutable emotion came and went in his mesmerizing whiskey-colored eyes. "Not with it going through probate and becoming court record." His broad shoulders flexing, he exhaled. "So do you think you can handle the gossip?"

She had endured worse, with the unforeseen breakup of her only serious romantic relationship. Not wanting to talk about what had been one of the most heart-wrenching times of her entire life, she tossed the ball back into his court. "You're the one with the big extended family. How are they all going to feel about us getting hitched for practical reasons?" The Lockhart clan put love and family above all else.

Briefly, his expression turned brooding. "I doubt they will like the way it's all come about. On the other hand—" he shrugged "—they've always wanted me to get married."

"To someone you barely know?"

"Well, first of all," he retorted, "they don't know how well I know you…or any other woman, for that matter. Second, I think they are smart enough not to weigh in on something that is essentially *our* private business."

Skye let out a tremulous breath. "And yet…" He still seemed concerned about something.

"It would probably be better if we tied the knot first and told everyone else about it afterwards," he told her.

"You want to *elope*?"

He kept his eyes locked with hers. "Makes more sense than anything else under the circumstances, don't you think?"

It did. And yet… "I don't want to go to J. P. Randall's Bait and Tackle Shop," she blurted out before she could stop herself. "Even if it is apparently *the place* for a quickie wedding in Laramie County."

Travis grinned. "Yeah, one of my sisters, Mackenzie, first tied the knot there."

"What do you mean '*first*'?" Skye asked, stifling a surprised laugh.

"My parents threw her and Griff a surprise wedding later."

Interesting. Skye tried to recall what she knew about the rest of the Lockhart-family nuptials. "Your sister Faith got married at the Laramie Gardens Assisted-Living Center, didn't she?" That wedding had been the talk of the town the Christmas before. Willa and Walter had used the situation as an example of what incredible happiness could result when two people came together for someone or something else. In Faith's case, foster baby Quinn.

Travis nodded. "Yes, but Faith worked there, and the residents insisted—so it made sense because she wanted everyone to be there to witness her special day."

"Is that what you want? If our situation were ideal? All your friends and family present?"

"No. I'm not a hoopla kind of guy. I think my parents know that."

"Then that makes two of us." Sighing, Skye paused to consider. "I think we could probably get a marriage license at the San Angelo courthouse without word getting out. But that still would leave us the question of where we make it official after the obligatory seventy-two-hour waiting period."

His eyes lit up with sudden inspiration. In that instant, she knew why Walter and Willa had trusted him so much. "Leave that part to me," he said.

Travis went over to see his brother Noah that same evening. At eight thirty, he expected Noah's three daughters—twins Avery and Angelica, age three, and Lucy, age eight—to be in bed for the night, and they were.

However, their harried dad's day looked like it was far from over.

He still had work spread out over the big L-shaped desk he had installed in the main living area adjacent to the playroom. The kitchen beyond still bore the remains of the evening meal. Piles of what appeared to be clean laundry were strewn across the sofa.

"How are things going?" Travis asked as Noah ushered him in and shut the door behind them.

His brother squinted. "Did you come over here to criticize or lend a hand?"

Guilt flashed through Travis. He hadn't checked in on his widowed brother nearly as often as he should have. "Pitch in, as always. Where do you want me to start?"

Noah grunted in response.

"Dishes it is, then!" Travis stalked into the kitchen, where the leftovers from a kid-friendly meal remained.

"Trying to butter me up for something?" Noah asked.

Travis loaded the dishwasher with the skill of a kid who'd been assigned the chore many times. "Why would you think that?" he asked innocently.

"The fact you're here at all?"

Travis put the last of the dishes in, then turned to face his younger brother. "Well, there is something..."

"I'm listening."

"Remember years ago, when you got ordained as a

minister online so you could officiate at your friend's wedding in California?" he asked.

"Yeah."

"Is that licensure still good?"

"Yes. Why?" Noah eyed him suspiciously. "You know someone who needs married in a hurry?"

Four days later, marriage license and required paperwork in hand, Travis and Skye waited on the porch of the Winding Creek ranch house. Noah had agreed to come by to help them out after he dropped his girls off at school in town.

He was fifteen minutes late.

Skye, who'd already had to get someone to cover the first four hours of her nursing shift at the Laramie Community Hospital CCU, had to be at work in forty-five minutes. She paced back and forth on the front porch of the ranch house, wringing her hands in front of her. "He *is* coming, isn't he?"

Travis set the paperwork on the table, along with the jewelry box containing their rings and a bouquet of pink, yellow and white roses.

Why Travis had shown up with flowers this morning, Skye didn't know. This was a formality. Nothing more.

Certainly nothing romantic.

"Should we call him?" she asked nervously.

Travis chided her with a look. "He said he'd be here. Must have gotten held up."

"Should we check?"

Travis edged closer, his brisk masculine scent washing over her. He, too, was dressed for work in a tan shirt, dark jeans and boots. She was wearing navy scrubs, with a long-sleeved white thermal T-shirt beneath and cushioned sneakers made for a long day on her feet. Her brunette locks had been swept up in a clip on the back of her head.

Her goal had been to make this like any other day.

Travis was clearly trying to do the same while simultaneously taking care of all the "wedding details" for the both of them so she wouldn't have to worry about it. An effort she appreciated.

"Give him five more minutes," he said more gently.

Three minutes later, Noah's big SUV rumbled up the drive. He parked in front of the ranch house, then got out. His hair was rumpled. He did not appear to have had time to shower, and he needed a shave.

"Everything okay?" Skye couldn't help but ask.

"Before-school wardrobe crisis, times three." Travis's brother grimaced. "So. You two still going to do this?"

"Have to," Travis said.

Skye nodded. "It was Walter and Willa's last wish."

She wasn't surprised to see that Noah, who had tragically lost his wife two years before, appeared to understand all too well about unfulfilled dreams and the wish that something could be done about it, too.

"Not to worry. We'll take the short version," Travis joked, handing her the bouquet and one ring. He palmed the other.

Noah looked them over, taking in their unconventional clothing with something akin to resigned disapproval. "Yeah, well, okay. Just understand, for my own peace of mind, I have to do this right."

He motioned for them to stand in front of him and opened up the small book he held in his hands. With the November sunshine bathing them in soft autumnal light, he said, "We are gathered here together to unite Skye McPherson and Travis Lockhart in holy matrimony…"

And just that suddenly, this whole situation got very real.

Chapter Three

Finally, the vows were over. Travis breathed a sigh of relief. Skye did the same. She had to get to the hospital to relieve the person covering for her, so after she and Travis had signed the official papers where directed, she thanked Noah for his help, paused for the quick photo he insisted on taking of them and left immediately afterward, wedding bouquet still in hand.

Still feeling shell-shocked by what had just transpired, Travis offered to make coffee.

"Sounds good." Noah followed his brother into the dogtrot cabin that had been Travis's residence up till now. Starting this evening, he knew he would have to sleep in the main house—with Skye.

The master bedroom had been completely emptied out after the Braelochs passed, as per their instructions;

everything had been donated. Another bedroom served as a storage locker, loaded with boxes. Skye occupied the only other suite.

Luckily, there was a hall bath he could use, along with a small guest room with a bed, dresser and nightstand already in it. So he and Skye would not be tripping over each other.

At least, that was what he kept telling himself. The last thing he needed was to see her in sexy disarray.

"So, when are you going to tell the family?" Noah asked, settling into a leather chair.

Travis put a coffee pod in the single-cup brewer. Hit Start. "When we're out at the Circle L Ranch on Thanksgiving Day."

The aroma of fresh-brewed coffee filled the rough-hewn two-room cabin. "You sure you want to wait until then?"

He handed a steaming mug to his brother. Shrugging, he made himself a cup, too. "It's only three days from now. That way we can tell everyone at once and be done with it."

Noah considered this. "You going to mention the will?"

Travis paused to take a long draught of the extra-strong brew. "Probably not then."

Noah—who had eloped during his first year in college and caught hell for it—lifted a brow.

Travis blew out a breath. "Obviously, I'll want to tell Mom and Dad before it goes through probate, which won't be until next Monday."

Noah silently sipped his coffee.

Finding he needed a sounding board, Travis asked

the brother he was closest to, "Think I'm making a mistake?"

Noah inclined his head. "I understand you have to do what you have to do."

"Is that why you had us seal our vows with a handshake instead of the usual kiss? Which, by the way, could easily have been a peck on the cheek."

Noah studied him with a half smile. "You could have kissed her, anyway."

Travis might have, except for the fact that the last time—the *only* time—they had ever let their instincts take them in that direction, it had ended in embarrassment and regret. He pushed away the memory of her soft lips and silky body. The perfect way their bodies fit.

"I'm pretty sure she would have preferred I not."

"Probably best," Noah ruminated. "Your relationship is going to get complicated enough as it is without bringing anything as risky as sex into it."

He was definitely right about that.

Theirs was an arranged marriage. Embarked upon to fulfill Willa and Walter Braeloch's last request. Nothing more.

As long as he and Skye both remembered that, Travis figured, they'd both be fine.

Three blissfully uneventful days later, Skye was busy in the ranch house kitchen when Travis walked through the back door, an armload of firewood in his arms.

He had been splitting logs since early that morning, carting some off to the dogtrot cabin, where most of his stuff still remained, and now bringing the remainder in here.

Glad they had settled into a platonic "roommates" routine with nary a hitch, she tossed him a casual half smile. "You worried about the weather?" she asked, scooping cooked sweet potato out of the skins.

He deposited the kindling into the metal wood bucket next to the fireplace, then came back to the kitchen to roll up his sleeves and wash his hands. "If the winter storm hits tomorrow morning like they are predicting, we could lose power. I want to make sure we have heat." He settled next to her with his hip braced against the counter and arms folded in front of him. Like her, he was not wearing his wedding band, though they had agreed that right before they made the announcement, they would slip them on.

Travis looked curious about what she was up to as well. "Is that for the dinner at my mom and dad's?"

"Yes. I ran into your mom at the hospital yesterday."

He lifted a brow.

"She was assisting a family who had a grandparent in the CCU."

His shoulders relaxed in relief. "Right."

Which made Skye wonder how her new husband would react if his family did not approve of what they had done. Never mind why.

"She told me how happy everyone was that you were bringing me as your guest. I offered to bring whatever was needed, and she mentioned no one had yet signed up for the sweet potato casserole."

He nodded and said nothing more.

Wondering what he was holding back, she said, "What's that look?"

His expression grew even more distant. "Nothing."

Yeah, right. One thing Skye really hated was people playing games with her. If they had something to communicate, she wanted them to simply do so, instead of expecting her to magically read their minds. "Come on… just spit it out already."

"Fine." He blew out a breath. "It's just… I don't really like sweet potatoes."

Was that all? A combination of oddly hurt feelings and irritation surging through her, Skye whisked in the remaining ingredients. "You don't have to eat it," she pointed out mildly before she could stop herself.

Leaning closer, he watched as she spread the fluffy mixture into two large casserole dishes and topped both with the crumble mixture of pecans, brown sugar, flour and, of course, more butter. "It would be weird if I didn't. Trust me, my siblings would notice if I didn't at least pretend to enjoy the food my date brought to the event."

She tingled all over at his nearness, the casual way he was invading her space, even if he didn't seem to realize it.

She shifted away from the tantalizingly masculine fragrance of his aftershave lotion. "You told them I was your 'date'?"

"No." Exhaling, he finally moved away. He roamed the kitchen restlessly, his broad shoulders flexing beneath his charcoal sweater. "I didn't qualify the situation one way or another. They just jumped to that assumption."

And clearly, he didn't like it.

Nor did she, really, when people formed conclusions regarding her love life.

Not that she and Travis were in love or ever would be.

Forcing herself to get back to the problem at hand, she slid the dish into the oven, then turned back to him. Winking, she teased, "Well, then I guess when it comes time for you to eat the dish I'm making, we'll find out how tough a cowboy you really are."

She grinned at him. He grinned back.

"Aww…" He looked her up and down, taking in the dark apron she had tied on over her pretty fall dress with a lazy insouciance that electrified her. His gaze lingered on her hair, her cheeks and lips. "You don't feel sorry for me?" he joked right back.

She shook her head, wishing he weren't looking at her with raw desire in his eyes—and that she suddenly didn't want to kiss him so much. "Not at all…"

That seemed to please him.

"You going to be ready to leave at noon?" he asked.

And just like that, the holiday clock started counting down.

"Have you met all of my family members?" Travis asked while he drove the short distance to the Circle L Ranch.

Skye took a moment to consider. "Well, of course I know your mom from her work as a social worker at the hospital. As for your four sisters… I met Jillian when I went over to pick up some of her antique roses for Willa. I've been to Emma's custom-boot store in town. Faith works at Laramie Gardens, so I was introduced to her when I took Willa over to see Nessie Rogers when she broke her hip and was recuperating there. And I met Mackenzie when Griff dropped off some legal papers for Willa and Walter last year."

She thought about the men in his family. "I haven't met your dad."

Travis smiled, his eyes lighting up with customary good humor. "He's a really great guy. You'll like him."

If Robert Lockhart was anything like his son Travis, she knew she would.

Realizing she had her hands full navigating the holiday celebration ahead, Skye continued thoughtfully, "I know Gabe from his work as a physician in the ER. And I met Cade when one of the baseball players he coaches sprained his wrist and was brought into the hospital last month."

Travis's hands competently circling the wheel, he probed her with a quick, assessing glance. "Do you know Faith's husband, Zach Callahan?"

Skye told herself it was the heat blowing out of the vents in the cab making her sweat. "Is he the former navy SEAL who now does custom cabinetry work?"

He nodded. "What about Jillian's husband, Cooper Maitland?"

Skye thought. "I met him very briefly. He was wrangling their three toddler daughters when I was paying Jillian for the antique roses Willa wanted planted last spring." Her throat ached at the memory of the good time they'd had while Willa directed, Skye did the work and Walter cheered on them both.

Catching the shift in her mood, Travis sent her a compassionate glance, letting her know he still had those moments of unexpected grief welling up, too. He reached over to briefly touch her wrist, then cleared his throat, returning his attention to the road. "What about Emma's husband, Tom Reid?"

She nodded, thinking about their delightful kindergarten-age triplets. "Austin, Bowie and Crockett were all in the store 'helping out' the day I purchased my boots." It was clear Emma and Tom both adored them. "Their dad was supervising. They had a cute dog with them."

Travis chuckled, obviously familiar with the gorgeous Australian labradoodle. "Buttercup."

"Right."

Circle L Ranch came into view. Travis turned into the driveway, and moments later, his truck moved beneath the wrought iron sign. Split-rail fences lined the long drive up to the main house. The sprawling two-story abode had a white stone exterior with a charcoal-gray roof and cedar shutters. And, in Skye's opinion, the modern Western farmhouse perfectly suited the renowned ten-thousand-acre cattle ranch. Clearly, they weren't the first to arrive.

Pickups and SUVs were already parked along the circular drive, one behind the other, in close proximity to the front door.

"Since you know a lot of my family already, then

this gathering shouldn't be too overwhelming," Travis said as he found a spot and shut off the engine.

She knew she could socialize with everyone, no problem. Their marriage announcement was something else indeed. Skye was nervous about that. But it had to be done, and Travis was right, it would be best to tell everyone all at once.

She inhaled and squared her shoulders as they strode side by side across the pavement to the front door, each of them carrying one of the two covered casserole dishes she had prepared.

"Welcome!" Robert said, letting them in.

The house—which had a beautiful rustic modern-farmhouse vibe inside as well—smelled deliciously of roasting turkey and sage. The sounds of a football game on TV, mingled with women's chatter in the kitchen, and the excited voices of the small children playing together in the family room, permeated the air.

Travis formally introduced her to his dad, who briefly relieved them of their dishes while they removed their coats and hung them in the front-hall closet. "Where should we put these?" she asked once the initial pleasantries had concluded.

Robert's smile broadened. "That's a question for my wife, Carol." He led her into the kitchen.

Skye was greeted as warmly as she'd expected. "I'm glad you could join us," Carol said with a look of sympathy and understanding. The rest of the women seemed to feel the same. And suddenly, Skye knew. Travis had been mistaken in his assumptions—at least when it came to the women in the Lockhart clan. They all thought Travis had brought her here, not because he was romantically interested in her, as he had assumed, but because Walter and Willa had recently passed and she had nowhere else to go. Thus, they all thought his invitation had been borne of pity. And now they felt sorry for her, too. Which was the last thing she ever would have wanted.

She wondered how they would feel when they realized he had brought her here to announce their elopement. Would they think he had briefly lost hold of his senses and married her out of some misguided sense of pity, too?

After leaving Skye to get better acquainted with the women—who had to be a much easier audience than the men he was currently entertaining—Travis helped his brothers bring the extra tables and chairs into the dining room. "We were wondering when you would finally get around to asking your ranch mate out," Cade teased.

"It's not a date," Gabe corrected, with the assurance of the eldest son.

A date would be easier to explain, Travis thought, already dreading the moment when he had to make the big announcement and see the looks on his family's faces.

Helping Noah move the big table to make room for the extra seating, Griff kept mum, as did Noah.

Grateful for his brother and brother-in-law's silence, since they alone knew the truth to be revealed, Travis went back to get the extra folding chairs.

Faith's husband, Zach, studied Travis with the highly developed intuition of a former navy SEAL. "Or…is it more than that?" he drawled.

Not sure what to say, Travis paused.

Emma's spouse, Tom, sent his in-laws a quelling glance. "I think it's just nice she's here," he said kindly.

"Agreed," Robert declared.

Everyone nodded. And to Travis's relief, that was that. At least for the time being.

Talk turned to the football games slated to be played that day and the predicted winter weather. The kids all wanted snow. Lots of it! But the adults were worried about the wintry mix of sleet and ice, which could bring about power outages. Since most everyone lived out in rural Laramie County, they all knew if the lines went down, they could be without electricity for twenty-four hours or more.

Every time Travis caught a glimpse of Skye—who was hanging out in the kitchen with the other women, helping to pull the meal together—she looked relaxed and at ease. It was only as everyone headed into the big formal dining room that he saw her begin to tense.

"Doing okay?" Travis whispered in her ear as he held out a chair for her.

She turned and gave him a dazzling smile that did not match her eyes. "Absolutely!"

Tradition had everyone holding hands as grace was said. When he took Skye's hand in his, he couldn't help but think how soft and delicate it felt. Or remember how deftly her fingertips had glided over his skin…

How hotly they had kissed.

For the first time, he wondered if they would be able to hold to their agreement to keep their marriage strictly platonic.

Several hours later, the holiday gathering began to die down. Travis made his way to Skye's side. "About ready?" he asked her quietly.

He reached into his pocket, slid on his ring and then slipped her the other one. She put the gold band on her finger just as surreptitiously. "I'm going to let you take the lead," she told him quietly.

"No problem," he whispered back. "Everyone! I have an announcement to make!"

Oh, dear, Skye thought as her knees began to quake and her head began to spin.

All eyes turned to him. With his customary confidence, Travis continued, "Skye and I eloped."

There were only two people in the room who were not absolutely gobsmacked—the Braelochs' attorney, Griff. And Noah. A shocked silence reigned. "You... what?" his mother asked finally.

"We got married on Monday," Travis said, flashing a big boisterous grin at his family while wrapping an easy arm around Skye's waist. Which was good because the uncomfortable stares and lingering shock had made her knees shake even harder.

Something isn't right.

She had been feeling a little off all day. Initially, she had chalked it up to nerves; but now, with everyone staring at her and Travis as if they had lost their everlovin' minds, the weird feeling grew. Her quaking knees seemed to lose their strength.

She felt herself sway.

And then her world went black…

Chapter Four

Slowly, the darkness faded. The living room of the Circle L ranch house came into view.

"What happened?" Skye stared up at the circle of Lockharts around her. Gabe, the only other health professional in the room aside from herself, was holding her left wrist, taking her pulse. He had a stethoscope around his neck, his medical bag open beside him. Travis knelt on her other side, holding her right hand, looking concerned.

"You fainted," Gabe said.

Skye let out a shaky laugh. "Impossible." She pushed the words through trembling lips, astounded at how weak and thready her voice sounded, even to her own ears. "I never faint…"

Gabe squinted at her. "Well, you did."

Travis squeezed her fingers, looking impossibly tender and concerned. The way a newlywed husband should, she couldn't help but think. His care did not go unnoticed. His family, who just a few minutes before, had been regarding him with total shock and skepticism, now looked at him with approval.

Determined to regain her strength, Skye struggled to sit up. As she did, a new wave of dizziness swept over her. With a defeated groan, she sank back, this time feeling Travis's strong arms guiding her down.

"How can I help?" Travis asked.

Gabe continued monitoring her pulse. "Maybe some orange juice. And a pillow or two."

Emma and Mackenzie immediately went off to fulfill the requests. When they came back, Gabe and Travis slid the pillows beneath Skye's feet and calves, raising her legs above heart level.

As the blood flowed to her head, Skye felt instantly better. She could tell she was looking better, too, by the relaxed smiles and sighs of relief of those still protectively gathered around her. "So, this has never happened before?" Gabe asked, still in ER-doctor mode.

"No," Skye said quickly. Then realized that wasn't exactly true.

Not about to talk about that part of her life here and now, however, she inhaled deeply. "I'm not really the fainting type."

In fact, she had made it all the way through nursing school and eight years of clinical practice without once losing her composure.

With an airy wave of her hand, Mackenzie soothed, "Oh, everyone can faint, if the circumstances are right."

Cade's wife, Allison, did her best to console, too. "That's right. I passed out once in the grocery store when I was pregnant with our twins."

Pregnant...

Abruptly, the room fell silent. Skye knew what they all were wondering. Especially given their just-announced secret elopement. Luckily, everyone was way too polite to ask.

Travis was as poker-faced as could be, too. "Think you can sip a little juice now?" he asked gently.

Skye nodded and he helped her sit up. This time, there was no dizziness. "Juice sounds good," she said.

Getting out of there ASAP sounded even better.

"You sure you can walk?" Travis asked a few minutes later as he helped her with her coat.

Skye nodded. "I'm feeling fine now. The fresh air will do me good."

After they said goodbye to Carol and Robert, they eased out the front door to a flurry of further congratulations. At last, it was silent. Stars shone in the Texas night sky above as they walked past the long row of vehicles to Travis's truck.

He had his arm around her waist.

Just this once, Skye couldn't say she minded the proprietorial embrace. He eased her into the passenger seat, then circled around to climb in behind the wheel.

He turned to her as soon as he shut the door. "Are you sure you're okay? You're not getting sick or anything?"

She felt bad she had alarmed him, too. "I'm not getting sick."

He turned on the ignition. After a moment, lukewarm heat poured out of the vents. Hands resting atop the steering wheel, he just continued sitting there, staring straight ahead. "What about…?"

"What Allison said?"

He turned to look at her in that quiet, steady way she was already beginning to love. "Is there a chance you could be pregnant?"

Not unless the universe really has a wicked sense of humor. Skye swallowed. "We used condoms that one night we were together," she reminded him.

"I know." He turned on the headlights and pulled out into the driveway, heading back toward the road. "But nothing is foolproof."

He's right about that.

"When's the last time you…ah…" His voice trailed off uncomfortably.

Skye threw up her hands. "Had a period? I honestly can't remember. I've always been irregular."

"Oh." The single word hung heavily between them. His brow furrowed. "I don't suppose you have any of those at-home test kits around?"

She sighed. "No, unfortunately I don't. And because it's a holiday, there is nothing open in Laramie County this evening. But I can go to the superstore tomorrow and pick up one."

He nodded. "Probably a good idea." Without warning, Travis hit the brakes. "What the heck…" he said as the truck headlights illuminated the road in front of them. It didn't take long for her to see why he'd stopped in his tracks. In the middle of the street was a mud-covered dog, struggling to get all the way across the road before they could hit it.

Luckily, Travis was able to stop in time. Leaving the motor on, he opened the door and jumped out. Skye followed just as the dog collapsed.

Travis had always had a soft spot for animals. And right now, his heart went out to the shaking, half-starving beagle covered in mud and burrs. Skye looked equally distraught by the condition of the dog, who had no collar or identification of any kind. "I've got a wool blanket tucked behind the driver seat," he told her.

"I'll get it."

Once she returned, he managed to lift the shaking pup into his arms while Skye wrapped her in the wool blanket. "You okay with me taking her to Winding Creek?" he asked.

"Absolutely." They walked back to the truck. Skye climbed in first. She buckled her seat belt, and he handed her the bundled-up hound to hold.

"Poor thing must be lost," she murmured, stroking the poor pup's damp head without regard for the mud coming off in her hand.

Travis frowned. "Or dumped in the country."

A shiver went through her at the thought of this sweet beagle being cruelly abandoned. "Well, hopefully, that's not the case and she just ran off and has been struggling to find her way home."

Travis gave the pooch another glance, taking note

of how natural Skye looked snuggling the full-grown dog in her arms.

No doubt about it, she had a big heart and a fiercely protective maternal streak that he couldn't help but admire.

"We can take the dog to the vet in the morning to see if she has a microchip. In the meantime, we'll get her cleaned up and fed, and make sure she is safe for the night."

Skye peered beneath the blanket. "And most important, the burrs have to come out."

It took a good half hour and both of them to get the dog cleaned up once they got back to the ranch. Luckily, the dog tolerated the warm water and grooming process well. After they had gotten her out of the bath and finished drying her, Travis carried her downstairs.

Skye turned to him, her hair swept up in a loose, messy knot on the back of her head. She'd ditched the pretty dress she had worn to his family gathering and put on a pair of snug-fitting leggings and an oversize flannel shirt before they bathed the dog. Her cheeks were pink. She and the dog now both smelled like the fragrant shampoo she used to wash her own hair.

Since they didn't have any dog food, they improvised with a meal of scrambled eggs and broken-up pieces of plain toast. Because the dog still seemed a little anxious, they both sat on the kitchen floor with the exhausted hound. After gobbling up the food, she lapped up water thirstily, then came back to climb into Skye's lap, where she settled in, as if to go to sleep for the night.

Skye lovingly stroked the dog's floppy ears, her

soothing touch as gentle and loving as her personality. "I wonder how long she's been on her own."

Reminded of how fantastically Skye made love, Travis cleared his throat and forced himself to concentrate on the matter at hand instead of the hot memories that still haunted his dreams nightly.

"Hard to tell." Travis surveyed the dog's ribs, which were visible beneath the skin. "At least a few days, I'm guessing…"

The young dog looked at him with dark liquid eyes. Seeming to need his touch, she scooted closer so Travis could pet her, too. He complied, already half in love with the stray.

Warning himself not to get too involved with a dog not meant to stay with him long-term any more than Skye was, he rose. "It's going to be a busy morning. I better get her to bed."

"What's the latest on the storm?" Skye asked as she rose, too.

Travis pulled out his phone and checked the weather app. "The wintry mix is slated to start around noon." He saw the corners of her soft lips turn down. "Don't worry. I've got all-wheel drive on my truck."

"I know we have to get her to the veterinary clinic in town first thing tomorrow," Skye told him soberly, worry clouding her dark brown eyes, "but I still want to be home before any precipitation starts."

Home.

Funny how good that word sounded coming from her. Resisting the urge to haul her close for a good-night kiss, Travis simply said, "No problem."

* * *

The next morning, Dr. Sara Anderson-McCabe finished the canine's exam, then waved an electronic wand over the back of the lost pooch's neck and smiled. "Good news. This little darling not only suffered no lasting harm from her adventures on the road, but she is also microchipped!"

At the news, Travis went completely still. Skye's heart clenched. She felt elated and heartbroken all at once.

"Hang on while we see if we can get ahold of her owners and see if we can come up with a plan to re-unite them." Dr. Sara slipped out of the room.

Skye faced Travis across the waist-high exam table. Their little lost pup rested between them, panting lightly. Obviously, the pet had no idea what was going on.

Travis inhaled. "Well, that's good news, isn't it?" he said with what sounded like forced cheer.

Maybe if I hadn't already fallen head over heels in love with the cute beagle, Skye thought. Figuring there was no mourning what could not be changed—especially if this sweet dog they had rescued already belonged to someone else who loved her—she kept that thought to herself.

Thankfully, before long, the exam-room door opened. "Did you talk to the owners?" Travis asked the moment Dr. Sara walked in.

The vet nodded, her expression grim. "They don't want her back."

Skye gasped. *"Why not?"*

"Apparently, they purchased her with the idea of

training her to hunt. She doesn't have the aptitude, and last weekend, during a training trial, she got spooked and ran off. They spent half the day looking for her and finally had to give up and go home without her."

"So that's it?" Skye asked, indignant. "They're just going to abandon her?"

"They want us to see if we can find her another home," Dr. Sara replied. "I've already agreed—"

"We want her," Skye blurted out before she could stop herself.

The vet turned to Travis. Travis met Skye's eyes. Smiled. "We do," he told the vet, just as firmly.

Abruptly, Skye felt so happy, she was close to dissolving into tears.

Dr. Sara lifted a staying hand. "I recognize this is an emotional situation, and I'm happy you two are willing to help this little adorable pup out. But this is a big decision…" She glanced at the matching plain gold bands on their ring fingers. Apparently, having heard of their recent elopement, too. Which was no surprise. The news was already spreading through Laramie County like wildfire. "And clearly, you both have a lot going on already." She smiled. "Therefore, I think you might want to give it a month—or even longer, if you need it—to decide whether you want to permanently adopt her or not."

"She's already been through so much," Skye said emotionally. "I can't bear the thought of her going through Christmas not knowing whether she has a forever home or not!"

Travis reached over to squeeze her hand. "I concur."

"All right," Dr. Sara relented. "She can stay with you for now—and if, in a month or so, everything has gone well and you are ready to formally adopt her, you can sign the papers then."

Skye sighed with relief. Grinning, Travis asked the vet, "What's her name, by the way?"

"Luna."

Which, Skye knew, meant *goddess of the moon*.

"Seems to fit her," Travis murmured as Luna wagged happily, "given how beautiful she is."

Skye petted the pooch tenderly, her heart filling with love. "Appropriate, too," she said softly, exchanging relieved looks with Travis, "since we found her in the moonlight…"

Fifteen minutes later, they left the vet clinic, loaded down with dog food, dishes, a collar, leash, heartworm and flea medicine, and a booklet on how to care for a new rescue pet.

It was nine o'clock.

The storm was due to start around noon.

Travis started the truck. "Do you have to work this weekend?"

"Not until Sunday." Which would give her two whole days to get Luna settled in and completely adjusted to her new home.

Travis backed out of the space. "How are we set for groceries?"

"Probably could use a few things, in case we get iced in."

"Plus…" He looked at her meaningfully before turning onto Main Street.

"The pregnancy test." The words came out in a low, strangled tone. Funny how she had managed not to think about that for the last twelve hours or so.

They were silent, lost in their own thoughts as he continued driving.

She wasn't sure what she was hoping.

She had always wanted a husband and family of her own. But she had also pretty much given up on that ever happening.

Yet here she was, four days married. Possibly with a baby on the way.

Unbelievable…

Not that she really thought she was pregnant.

They had only been together one night. What were the odds, statistically? There was no telling what Travis was thinking. She only knew he was very quiet.

Too quiet?

Since they didn't want to leave Luna in the truck alone, when they finally reached the superstore at the edge of town, they agreed that Travis would stay with her while Skye ran in.

The store was packed with people gearing up for the winter storm. Skye hurried, but it was still a good thirty-five minutes before she got back to the car, carrying several bags of groceries.

"Get everything?" Travis asked.

Meaning, Skye thought, *the Test.*

"Yes," she nodded, trying not to flush. "Then home it is…"

A short while later, they arrived back at the ranch house. Seeing no reason to delay it further, Skye left Travis to put away the food and get Luna settled while she disappeared into the bathroom downstairs.

Three minutes later, she had the results.

Hands shaking, she walked back out into the hall to see him sitting on the staircase, hands clasped between his knees. "Well?" Travis said with an urgent, expectant look on his face.

"It's positive."

Chapter Five

Travis stared at the two red lines in the window of the pregnancy test. Skye had the back of the box for him to look at, too. Which said that the results were indeed positive. "We're going to have a baby?" He noted that she looked as stunned as he sounded. Which probably meant she had been telling herself that this was a false alarm, too. That her fainting at the exact moment they were telling his entire family about their elopement would be something they could chuckle over later...

Pink color flooding her cheeks, Skye inhaled deeply. "Apparently so."

"A baby," he murmured. The two of them were going to have a baby! The knowledge hit him like a tsunami. Acting on instinct, Travis swept her up and held her against him. She rested her arms on his shoulders and turned her face up to his.

The next thing he knew, her lips were parting. His head was lowering. And they were kissing as if there was nothing but this incredibly magical moment in time.

All he could think about was making wild, passionate love with her again. And he knew this baby they had made was not just going to immediately bring the two of them together in ways they had never anticipated when they said "I do." It would change their lives forever.

Skye hadn't intended to ever kiss Travis again—especially not now, when she was still so incredibly vulnerable. Falling victim once to his sexy masculinity had already turned her world upside down. She should be concentrating on what they were going to do about the baby they had just found out about instead of surrendering to the pent-up desire she had been feeling for quite some time.

But there was just something so damn exciting about Travis's embrace. She couldn't help but revel in the masterful feel of his lips on hers, the erotic sweep of his tongue, the warm cage of his powerful arms and the hard demand of his body pressed up against hers.

She had never been kissed with such smokin'-hot tenderness, never been held with such fierce possessiveness. And had never felt such need welling up inside her. She knew if she continued to let him seduce her into celebrating their news this way that she would eventually end up right back in bed with him.

Because the truth was, even if she did not want to admit it, she had always had a thing for him. How could she not? He was so sexy and masculine. So deliberate and determined in everything he did.

And what he was doing right now was tempting her into turning their marriage of convenience to one that included hot, wild sex. Which would be fine, she thought, if she felt they were ever going to fall in love. But that wasn't the deal they had made…

So Skye tore her lips from his, jerked in a breath and pressed a staying hand against his chest.

Slowly, reluctantly, he lifted his head. A complex array of emotions crossed his handsome face.

"We have to stop before it's too late."

To Skye's relief, her practical words were as effective as a bucket of cold water dumped over both their heads. Just as swiftly, the passion that had flared up between them faded.

"But you're happy, right?" Travis asked. His voice dropped to a husky rasp. "About the baby?"

He clearly was.

Was she?

How could she not be? When a baby—a family of her own—was all she had ever wanted.

And yet…

"If you're worried about me being a good dad, you needn't be," Travis said, misunderstanding the reason behind her unease.

She flushed as his eyes pierced hers with an intensity that rendered her breathless.

"I promise I'll make sure you both have everything you need, from here on out."

She'd heard those words before. Only to have them later taken back. She swallowed around the ache rising in her throat. "I don't want to be a burden."

"It's *our* child, Skye. Not just yours." He clasped her hand in his, giving her fingers a reassuring squeeze. "And you and our baby *could never* be a burden to me."

She stepped back, her fingers tingling, her insides feeling like they were ready to combust into flames. And all from just one brief touch. A hot kiss before that...

What would happen if they got a heck of a lot closer emotionally, too?

"I promise I will always be here for the two of you," he continued gruffly.

Swallowing hard, she went over to look out the front windows to check on the progress of the approaching storm, which seemed to be getting closer. "You say that now..."

He followed her, looking out at the thick gray clouds dominating the horizon. Then he turned to regard her quietly. "I mean it."

They were close enough she could feel the body heat emanating from his tall, strong frame. "You think you do. But I've been down this road before, Travis."

It took him a moment to understand what she was talking about. His eyes widened. "You were pregnant?"

Skye nodded, reluctantly admitting, "When I was living in Chicago a few years back."

"What happened?" He leaned in a little more.

"Initially, it was eerily similar to what's happening right now. Dex, the surgical resident I was dating at the time, was as shocked as I was—but happy and excited, too. He insisted we get married right away. I said yes because I loved him. Or at least thought I did."

His brown eyes shone with empathy. "It didn't work out well?"

Remembering how overwhelmed she had felt at the time, Skye shook her head. "He was from a wealthy family. His mother took over the wedding-planning." Frowning, she continued, "What would have been a quiet ceremony quickly zoomed into a formal event for 350 people. The invitations were just about to go out when I lost the baby."

He reached out and gently squeezed her hand. "I'm sorry."

Skye sighed, aware she couldn't help but still be a little bitter about what had happened next. She inclined her head, looking deep into Travis's eyes, curious what his reaction was going to be. "A day later, Dex called the whole thing off."

Travis did a double take. "A *day* later?" he echoed, looking like he wanted to track down her ex and read him the riot act.

Skye nodded, relieved that someone else found her ex's behavior utterly reprehensible. "Dex said there was no longer any reason for us to get married. And he thought we should go back to the way things had been."

Travis's broad shoulders relaxed slightly. "What did *you* want?"

"Honestly? I wanted for none of it to ever have happened. But at least, I thought, we still had each other, and there would be other babies in the future."

Travis assessed her with a look. He folded his arms in front of him. "I'm guessing it didn't work out that way."

Sadly, Skye shook her head. "Dex started making excuses not to see me." She jerked in a breath, wishing she still didn't feel so humiliated. "When I called him on it, he admitted he had never seen us as a forever kind of thing."

Travis's eyes darkened with a compassion and understanding that warmed her soul.

Making it easier for her to go on.

"So we cut short our misery and ended it. I felt like I needed a complete change of scenery to recover."

"Makes sense," he said in a low, gravelly voice.

Skye released a quavering breath. "So I moved to Texas."

Travis put his hands on her shoulders and rasped, "I'm sorry you went through all that. And for the record—" his lips compressed briefly into a cynical line "—your ex was a jackass."

Skye didn't know why hearing that from Travis helped. She only knew it did.

"But again," he told her heavily, his expression as genuine and honest as his low tone, "I would never do that to you."

Skye figured that was true. Personal honor was a huge deal in this part of Texas. For the Lockhart family, too.

Neighbors helped neighbors.

Family always stepped in to help out their own.

And marriage and children—well, they were the most precious of all.

Skye paused. "If I'm to be completely fair—I don't think Dex ever set out to hurt me. We just wanted different things. The baby we were going to have, the excitement and joy, united us temporarily."

"You don't think it would have kept you together for the long haul?"

She shook her head. "Sadly, no. My point is, I don't want *us* to make the same mistake."

Travis took her by the hand and led her over to sit on the couch. Their knees brushed as they settled into the comfy cushions together. He continued holding her hand. "Are you worried about losing this baby?"

She looked down at their entwined fingers. His were big and capable; hers, delicate. "The biggest risk is in the first trimester." Her free hand went to her middle, lingered protectively. "We conceived this child on August 20."

The night of Willa and Walter's joint memorial service.

He paused to do some quick calculations. "Which means you are past the twelve-week mark."

Skye nodded. "I'll still try to get in to see my ob-gyn next week."

His expression tender, he sat back in his chair. "Is it okay if I go with you?"

The independent side of her wanted to say no. But the co-parent in her knew she had to be fair from the get-go. "Yes," she said.

Travis smiled. "Great."

That settled, they shifted their attention to getting ready for the impending winter storm.

Half an hour later, enough firewood to get them through the storm was stacked next to the hearth in the living room. Travis was cleaning the ashes out of the fireplace and Skye had just gotten out the ingredients for sandwiches when a loud grinding sound permeated the downstairs. Then everything went silent.

She had moved the new dog bed they had made up for Luna from the living room to the kitchen so she wouldn't be alone, and the beagle seemed to be acclimating well. But now Luna sat up, ramrod straight, looking alarmed. Travis joined them a few moments later, his hair still windswept, his cheeks ruddy from the cold.

"What was that?" Skye asked.

He put his hand over one of the vents. Grimaced. "If I had to guess, the furnace."

"Oh no…"

"I'll go check." He grabbed his coat and the tool box, and went outside to the utility closet off the back porch. She followed, watching from just inside.

He fiddled with the ancient heat exchanger and pump for the next ten minutes.

Frowning, he returned.

"I think it finally bit the dust."

"What are we going to do?"

He turned his glance to Luna, then back to her again.

"The best thing to do would be for us all to move over to the cabin."

She slid him a look. "It's awfully small."

He narrowed his gaze. "It also has a working furnace."

The sleet was already starting to come down.

Telling herself they would be able to handle the close quarters without doing anything reckless, Skye relented. "I guess that's where we will ride out the storm, then."

Skye packed an overnight bag while Travis pulled his truck up to the front porch and transferred groceries to the rear passenger side. A stack of kindling went next. Then the dog food, dishes and pet bed.

Skye got her scarcely used winter boots and parka out of the front-hall closet and put them on, then knelt to pet the shivering beagle. "It's okay, Luna, darlin'," she murmured, knowing that if the drafts from the open door were too much for the still achingly thin rescue pet, the cold of an unheated house would be really miserable.

Travis was back. He had on his shearling-lined winter boots, Stetson and down jacket. "I'll carry her out," he said, all business. "Wait here."

She could see how slippery it was already getting.

As soon as Luna was settled, he came back for Skye, keeping a firm grip on her as she navigated the steps down to the pickup and directly into the cab.

Sleet was coming down hard.

It glistened on the brim of his hat and in the ends

of his hair as he drove the hundred yards to the dogtrot cabin.

She reached for the door handle. He shook his head, barking out gruffly, "Wait for me."

She wanted to argue that she was perfectly capable of managing a few sleet-covered steps. She also knew a fall in her condition would not be good. Travis was right. Better to err on the side of caution.

He helped her out, then went back for Luna before hustling them both into the cabin.

It was as dark and chilly as she'd expected it to be, given the fact he hadn't been living there for the last week. She turned on the lights while he brought everything in. She knelt next to Luna and looked around.

Like all dogtrots, the cabin was two-and-a-half-rooms wide and one-room deep, with a front porch that ran the entire length. The kitchen, living and dining areas comprised one room; the bedroom, the other—with a bathroom and laundry closet in between.

He had decorated it sparsely, with dark leather furniture and Southwestern rugs. She also noticed he had a desk beneath the window, with a laptop and printer, as well as a wall-mounted TV above the mantel.

Everything else was very masculine. Austere. It was very much a bachelor's lair.

Very much…*him*.

Travis came in and set the last of their stuff down, looking very much like the quintessential cowboy in full command. "That's it," he announced gruffly.

"What can I do to help?"

He went to the wall thermostat. Turned it up. "Rustle us up something to eat while I build a fire?"

The furnace came on with a satisfying purr. Skye shrugged out of her winter parka. "Coming right up."

Trying not to think about how cozy and somehow right this all felt, she put together a meal of premade potato soup and grilled ham-and-cheese sandwiches. By the time she had put everything on the table, Luna had settled onto her cushion and Travis had a fire crackling in the grate.

Their knees bumped as they sat opposite each other. Skye drew back. "What is the latest on the weather, do you know?"

He took his cell phone out of his pocket, tapped the weather-app icon. "Looks like we're going to get hit pretty hard with this sleet-snow combination through the night."

In Chicago, this would have been no big deal. They had plenty of salt and heavy equipment to deal with bad roads. But here, in Texas, where it barely snowed? The situation could be dire. "Accumulation?"

Travis's chiseled lips tightened in contemplation as he continued scrolling. "Maybe half an inch. Depends on how long it takes the ground to freeze."

Already way too physically aware of him, she shrugged and ate her soup. She could not let this situation send them back into each other's arms. No matter how bored or scared or cold they got.

"That's not so bad." Not when you compared it to the long, brutal winters she'd endured in the Midwest.

He put his phone down and concentrated on his

meal. "The temperature is going down to thirty by nightfall," he told her matter-of-factly.

"That sounds manageable, too."

"Until you realize it only takes a quarter of an inch of ice to bring tree branches down onto power lines."

And downed power lines mean no electricity, no heat. Their gazes intersected. "Oh."

After finishing his soup, he leaned back in his chair with a sigh of satisfaction. Next to the hearth, Luna snored. The moment drew out pleasurably. Attraction shimmered between them. "This the first time you've actually been in a west Texas ice storm?" he asked eventually.

Skye warned herself to stay focused, to not give in to the wish to see if their lovemaking would be just as fantastic the second time... "Yes." She regarded him pragmatically. "The last two winters here have been reasonably mild."

"Well, the precipitation will stop by morning, and it should be around forty by noon. So whatever we get in terms of snow or ice will melt then."

Skye told herself they could handle twenty-four hours of being shut in the dogtrot together without getting cabin fever. Especially when they had other issues to deal with.

"What are we going to do about the furnace in the ranch house?" she asked.

Travis ate the rest of his sandwich in a single bite. "We can try and get someone out here tomorrow, when the roads clear. But it probably won't happen until next week." Without warning, he put the heel of his hand against his forehead. Groaned.

"What is it?" she asked in alarm.

"The faucets." He was already up and out of his chair, heading for the door. He pulled on his down jacket and slapped his still-wet Stetson on his head. "I forgot to turn them to drip and open all the cabinet doors under the sinks!"

Skye and Luna both stood. "Why would you want to do that?" she asked.

"So the pipes don't freeze."

He shoved his feet back into the boots he'd left by the door. He knelt to lace them up.

Seeing her distress, he winked. "Don't worry. I'll take care of it and will be right back."

Skye's heart was pounding as she watched Travis zip up his winter jacket and duck out the door. She and Luna stood on the other side of the portal, watching him slip-slide his way down the steps. The frozen precipitation already coated the ground, looking slick and dangerous. When he reached his pickup, he climbed into the passenger side, pushed up the center console and then slid across the seat, shutting the door behind him.

Luna had picked up on her anxiety and now stood beside her—body tense, ears back, tail moving slowly at half-mast.

"See that, girl? He knows what he is doing," Skye murmured, shutting the door and heading over to the window, to continue watching.

Or does he? she wondered as the truck slowly fish-tailed its way toward the main house while the sleet came down heavier than ever. Several times on the hundred-yard journey, it seemed to lose all forward traction. Stalling out. Sliding backward.

Each time, she caught her breath. Each time, Travis handled the situation with skill. Until finally the truck reached the ranch house.

He parked a distance away from the porch steps, and she could just make out the driver's-side door opening. Her heartbeat accelerated as he appeared. Sticking close to the vehicle, he made his way around the front of the big quad cab, then abruptly disappeared.

"What...?" She blinked. Still not seeing him, she moved to another window for a better view.

Had he somehow made it into the house?

How could that have happened without her seeing him on the porch?

Where was he?

No. Wait. There he was! Moving slowly up the front steps. Carefully and strongly gripping the railing as he moved up, across and into the front door of the Victorian.

Skye breathed a sigh of relief and turned back to Luna. "See? He's fine. And will be back before we know it."

It was herself she was worried about. What was wrong with her? She wasn't usually such a nervous Nellie. Was it that she now knew he was her baby daddy and had therefore taken on a new importance in her life? Or was there something more at play here?

Skye shook off her romantic notions and headed back into the kitchen to do the dishes and put on a pot of coffee. And try to calm her frazzled nerves.

Yes, there was a fierce storm outside. But Travis had everything under control.

Meanwhile, she and Luna were safe. And so was the baby she carried inside her.

Chapter Six

Soaked to the bone and near-freezing, Travis finally made it back to the dogtrot cabin thirty minutes later.

"Oh my God, Travis! What happened to you?" Skye gasped, after yanking open the front door. "We need to get you out of those wet clothes before you get hypothermia."

Her experience as a registered nurse clearly coming into play, Skye sprang into action, her soft hands brushing over his skin as she divested him of his drenched coat, his equally wet flannel shirt, thermal undershirt and boots.

When her hands went to the fly on his jeans, he intercepted gruffly. "I can handle this. I'll just take a hot shower."

Color flooded her cheeks. "A hot shower is the worst

thing for you right now. It could stress your heart and lungs and lead to frostbite in your extremities. But you can certainly take one after we get you warmed up."

We. He liked the sound of that.

She moved past him and toward his bed, all brisk medical professional now. "Let me know if you need help. I'm going to gather up some blankets."

His teeth were still chattering. He couldn't recall the last time he'd been so damn cold. "Th-thanks, N-N-Nurse S-S-Skye."

Grinning, she returned just as he had stripped down to his boxer briefs. Her gaze swept over him, lighting fires everywhere it landed. And places where it hadn't. "Are those wet?"

He nodded. The damn slush had soaked into everything he wore.

She wrapped a blanket around his shoulders. "Then it has to go, too." She patted him on the shoulder reassuringly. "Meanwhile, I'll get you something warm to drink."

The adrenaline that had propelled him thus far still going strong, he nodded back at her, stripping off his briefs as she walked away. "Thanks."

She returned, exuding kindness. "This will help."

She was helping.

He inhaled the inviting aroma of fresh-brewed coffee. She watched as he quaffed the cup, then gave him a refill. Taking him by the hand, she led him over toward the fire. Then, with his help, she pushed the sofa closer to the hearth. Luna was curled up on her dog bed, watching him. A wool lap blanket was looped over the back of the cushions.

Skye wrapped another blanket from his bed around his shoulders, then guided him onto the sofa and settled beside him. She tucked the lap blanket over him. "Better?" she asked.

"Much." Although he was still cold, his teeth had stopped chattering. The warmth from the fireplace was helping, too.

"Tell me what happened," she insisted with the same tender, loving care.

It had been a long time since he had been fussed over by a woman, and never quite like this. Was this what it would be like to really be married to her? And why wasn't that an unwelcome idea anymore?

She leaned forward urgently. "I saw you disappear from view—or at least, I thought I did, when you first got out of the truck."

So she had been watching over him.

"Did you fall then?" she pressed. Wrapping her arm around his shoulders, she pulled him against her soft warmth. "*Before* you went into the ranch house?"

"Yes." The spill would have been embarrassing as hell had it not been so damn scary and unsettling. Figuring she had a right to know, he turned to her and said, "When I got out of the truck and started around the front, I unwittingly stepped on a solid patch of ice, and my feet went out from under me." He inhaled and drank more coffee before forcing himself to go on. "The next thing I knew, I had the breath knocked out of me and I was lying all the way under the truck."

Skye's hand flew to her heart. "Oh, Travis!"

He frowned, recalling the danger he'd inadvertently put himself in. Danger that could have led to her getting hurt, too, had she come outside looking for him. "Had I not managed to catch hold of the bumper with my left hand on the way down—well, let's just say it kept me from sliding any further."

She looked horrified. Her forearm still pressing against the soft swell of her breasts, she asked, "How'd you get out?"

"I eventually bear-hugged the tire closest to me and managed to swivel around and push off with my feet till I could use the other tire as leverage. Then I pushed my way out from under the truck and eventually got back on my feet."

She bit her lip "Were you scared?"

"More like shaken up. And stunned."

She peered at him closely, her deepening concern evident. "You didn't hit your head or anything, did you?"

"No. It happened so fast, I think my entire body took the brunt of the fall rather than just one part. And my jacket provided some cushion for my back and shoulders, too."

"Thank heaven for that."

She reached over and touched his face. "Feeling warmer?"

"Getting there."

She took his mug. "I'll get you some more coffee. Maybe heat up another container of refrigerated soup, too, if you'd like."

"Sounds great. Thanks."

He watched her move about his small kitchen, amazed at how graceful and feminine she was. It didn't seem to matter if she was doing chores or caring for a rescued dog, or him. She was just so gentle and appealing.

She returned, oblivious to the effect she was having on him. "It should just take a few minutes."

Acutely aware of his nakedness beneath the blankets, he accepted the third cup of coffee she gave him. Judging by the new pink in her cheeks, she was suddenly cognizant of the disparity in their clothing, too.

Figuring if showering were out, then putting the moves on her had to be, too, he willed the blood out of his lower extremities. "You don't have to babysit me."

She glanced at Luna, who was still curled up on her cushion, watching him closely. Skye hovered next to him, teasing, "Our dog thinks I do."

But she went back to the stove to check on the soup. Gave it a stir. "Did you get everything done inside the ranch house that you needed to do?"

Travis nodded, trying not to notice how lovely she was in the soft afternoon light pouring into the cabin. Or think about how much he wished the situation were different. That they could start fresh and make love for all the right reasons this time.

"I took care of all the faucets and opened all the cabinet doors where there were pipes."

She stirred the soup again, turned up the heat beneath it. Her hair was in a knot, silky tendrils escaping every which way. "How was the temperature in the ranch house?"

"The thermostat said sixty degrees."

She turned to him in alarm. "It's dropping fast."

He cast a look outside. The way the storm was building, it was only going to get worse. "The whole place needs new energy-efficient windows."

"That's an expensive proposition."

He nodded. His experience as a handyman coming into play, he guesstimated, "About twenty thousand dollars to do the whole house."

Skye poured soup into a large mug and brought it over to him, then sank down on the sofa beside him. "That would eat up quite a bit of the money Willa and Walter put aside. If we could even get the fund administrator to agree it was a necessary improvement. Especially when it might be sold and/or torn down in a few months."

She spoke so casually about letting the place go. He'd felt the same, initially. However, living in the main house with her this past week—taking her to Thanksgiving dinner with his family and seeing her interact with them, knowing she was now carrying their child—had opened up his eyes to other possibilities.

To maybe wanting to stay at Winding Creek beyond the 120 days.

It was way too soon to be thinking like that, though, Travis reminded himself as he ate more of the hot, delicious soup. It warmed him even more than the coffee had.

"On the other hand," Skye mused, staring into the

flames in the hearth, "making a substantial improvement like that might be a way to draw in the kind of buyers Walter and Willa always wanted to see purchase the ranch. So making the ranch house a lot more energy efficient might be a very good thing."

Irritated to find himself in the same situation that had caused his only other serious relationship to go bust, he shrugged. "We should probably talk to some Realtors about the best way to proceed."

They would know the wisest move. Thereby taking the burden of decision-making and potential disagreement off him and Skye.

Her expression serious, she nodded. "I'll get right on it."

Skye spent the rest of the afternoon researching Realtors who specialized in Texas ranches. Travis waited until the danger of overtaxing his body had passed, then had a shower and got dressed in warm, dry clothes. Try as he might, though, he couldn't stop thinking about what had happened earlier—especially since the freezing precipitation continued to pour down from the skies. Icy rain one minute, sleet the next, then bursts of snow and fierce winds and back to sleet.

His truck and the ground were covered with at least half an inch of the treacherous mixture. He could see the shrubbery and other plants around the front of the dog-trot cabin suffering under the icy weight, too. Luckily, most were dormant. Otherwise, they wouldn't survive.

"Are you okay?" Skye asked finally, peering over at him as he got a couple of burger patties out of the freezer for their dinner and set them in a cast-iron skillet. "I mean, you don't have frostbite anywhere, do you? Or chest pain? Shortness of breath?"

And there she went. Back to being a nurse.

"No. Everything is fine. Nothing to worry about," he told her thickly.

She rose and came closer. "Are you sure?"

She had been resting her cheek on one upraised fist while searching the internet. A red mark remained on the left side of her face. He had a strong urge to gently caress her soft skin until the mark dissipated. Or better yet, take her in his arms and kiss her until all her questions faded.

Knowing neither action was a viable one, he turned away and took out a package of frozen fries, then added them to a baking sheet. "What do you mean?"

She got out the kibble and filled the food and water bowls for Luna. The dog ambled over. Skye gave her a gentle pat of encouragement, waiting until the beagle started to eat, then straightened and sauntered toward him once again. "You look like something is bothering you."

Not sure he wanted to talk about it in depth—yet knowing he had to give her something, or she would likely just keep asking questions—he waved off her concern. "I'm just thinking about my parents."

Skye blinked. "Carol and Robert?"

He shook his head. "Before them. My birth parents. I never understood how they could have done what they did the night they died. Until today."

Skye pulled the rest of the fixings for the burgers out of the fridge. "What happened to them?"

Grief swept through him once again. "Our home was struck by lightning in the middle of the night during a summer storm."

The color left her face.

Feigning a matter-of-factness he still couldn't really feel, Travis robotically went on reciting the way-too familiar details: "They got me and all seven of my siblings out and to a house across the street. The heavy rain had put out the flames on the roof. The fire department wasn't there yet."

Her hand stalled as she reached for a red onion. "Don't tell me they went back in."

He steeled himself against the painful memory. "There was a safe in the den, off the front door. It contained all our important papers and the jewelry my mother had inherited from her mother. They thought it would be okay. It was just going to take a minute."

Skye came over to take his hand in her gentle grip. "But it wasn't."

"The gas water heater was located in the attic. A spark from the lightning strike ignited it. It blew up, and the house collapsed on top of them, with us all watching."

She grasped his forearms, gazing up at him. "Oh my God, Travis."

He let her take him all the way into her arms to comfort him with a heartfelt embrace. Unfortunately, the gesture wasn't something he could return. Not when he still felt so numb inside. Eventually, she let him go. Stepped back. Waited for him to continue.

He shoved a hand through his hair and forced himself to continue. "All this time, I've been so angry with them for putting material things that could be replaced ahead of their safety and the future of their eight kids. For acting foolishly and leaving us orphaned."

"And you've resented the hell out of them for all that," she said, her gaze glimmering sympathetically.

Travis nodded as their eyes met and held a long empathetic moment. "But now… I think they must have felt the way I did this afternoon," he went on grimly, trying not to think about what could have happened had he smacked his skull on the driveway and sustained a major head injury. Or been unable to figure out a way to get out from beneath his vehicle before hypothermia overtook him…

Not to mention the fact that his careless impulsivity could have left *his* baby without a parent, too. And how ironic would that be, considering how judgmental he had been all these years…

"Now, you know that your parents were just acting on adrenaline," she sympathized. "Doing what they felt needed to be done in the crisis."

Glad she understood the complicated nature of his feelings and didn't seem to be judging him for his previous intolerant attitude, he nodded. Her eyes filled. Holding his hand tighter, she whispered, "What happened after that?"

He let out a rough breath, making no effort to camouflage his sorrow. "We were all split up into different

foster homes, until Robert and Carol were able to re-
unite us, one by one, and adopt us all."

She let out a soft empathetic sound. "Thank heaven
for the Lockharts!"

Travis agreed completely. "They've got the biggest
hearts of anyone I've ever known."

She leaned closer. Still listening. "How long were
you in foster care?"

"A little over two years. I was the last one adopted."

Finally, she let his hands go. It felt odd not to be holding on to her. "That must have sucked," she murmured.

It had. Figuring he had shown enough of his weak
side, he moved back to the stove, checking on the fries,
turning the heat back up under the burgers. "It was
okay." He added seasoning to the patties. "No one was
cruel to me. I just got moved around a lot."

She went back to the dinner prep, too. "Was there
any particular reason for that?"

"My social worker used to chide me for being so
difficult and aloof."

"Do you think that was a fair assessment?"

Damn, she was beautiful in her red sweater, jeans
and shearling-lined UGGs; her hair twisted in that
loose, sexy knot.

Her eyes such a pretty dark chocolate hue.

"Maybe. I don't know." He resisted the urge to take
her in his arms, pull her close and kiss her until all
these sad memories went away and all he felt was the
two of them, their warm bodies entangled.

She studied him from beneath the thick fringe of
her lashes. "Were you rude to people?"

Good question. "More like…uninterested in bonding with anyone. I missed my siblings. I wanted my old life back. Not something new. So I decided to carry on alone."

He plated their dinner and brought it to the table.

Skye handled the drinks and the condiments. "I get it. I didn't want to bond with my foster family, either," she said as they started to eat. "When I knew I was only going to leave…"

He glanced out the window at the mix of snow and rain still coming down in sheets. On the trees, *at least* a half an inch of ice had now formed. Not good. Not good at all.

Skye, however, was focused only on what was going on inside the cabin. "And now here we are…" She lifted her milk in a toast, and he clinked glasses with her, surprised at how much better he felt.

Smiling with a mixture of ruefulness and joy, she went on to say, "Two ex-foster kids married in name only and expecting a baby."

After dinner, they did the dishes together, then bundled up and took Luna outside. Although it was still sleeting heavily, Skye was relieved to see that the eighteen or so inches of porch floor directly next to the house was still dry, thanks to the overhang of the porch roof. So they waited there together, watching and murmuring encouragement while Luna navigated the slippery steps, her paws and nails giving her cleat-like traction. As soon as she'd taken care of business, she returned to the porch, drenched, shivering and wanting to go back inside.

Skye and Travis accommodated her.

The evening stretched ahead of them. The cabin was suddenly way too small and cozy, his presence far too strong and masculine.

It was a moment like this—when they had let the unexpected intimacy of a situation and their heightened emotions take over—that had gotten them into trouble in the first place.

She pushed away the yearning to feel even closer to him, resurrecting the barbed wire fence around her heart. "Want to watch some TV?"

"Sure." Looking relieved that she'd offered him a distraction from the awareness shimmering between them, Travis picked up the remote and switched it on. Static appeared on the screen. He tried several more channels, then frowned.

"Satellite is out," he said, as a loud snap sounded, followed by a great big thump that seemed to shake the ground. Simultaneously, all went black. The only light in the entire cabin came from the fire.

"And so is the power."

Chapter Seven

"We've got to be practical here," Skye said several hours later.

Thanks to the news alerts on their cell phones, they'd learned all of Laramie County was without electricity. The storm would continue until dawn, with major icing overnight.

Luckily, the sun was expected to warm things up by noon Saturday. That and the forecasted forty-degree temperature would melt the ice.

"The cabin is already getting really cold. And we only have four blankets between us—two of which are lap blankets."

His motions practiced and relaxed, Travis knelt to add another log to the fire. The hearth was warm; Luna was cozy and sleeping peacefully in her dog bed. He stirred up the flames. "You can have them all," he told her with his customary chivalry. "You'll be warm enough if you put them all on the bed."

"But what about you?" she returned heatedly. "You need to be comfortable, too!"

The corners of his eyes crinkled. "I'll be fine."

The wind was howling as the sleet continued to fall. The majority of the cabin had a distinct chill. "I don't want you to be miserable," Skye murmured. And he would be if he were too cold. They both would be. Because then, she would feel really guilty.

Irked at his stubbornness, she continued, "Plus, you already had one episode of near-hypothermia today."

He rubbed his hand over his jaw, then stood, towering over her once again. Something flickered in his expression, then disappeared. "I agree. That wasn't fun. But as you can see, I'm fine now and have been for hours."

But will he continue to be? Although he was still in the thermal long-sleeved tee, flannel button-up, jeans and wool socks he'd put on after his shower and looked to be just fine, she wasn't faring as well. She'd already had to don her winter jacket and gloves, and was now thinking about putting on a knit cap as well.

They needed a plan that would get them both comfortably and safely through the night.

"Then how will you stay warm?"

He shrugged. "I'll wear my coat, too."

She shivered beneath his continued scrutiny. "Where will you sleep?"

"Sofa."

Was he serious? The oversize love seat was not big enough to comfortably accommodate his six-foot-two frame!

"Or—" She drew a deep breath, watching him pace to the window to have a look outside. "We could both share the bed."

That caught his attention. His head whipped around. "As friends," she clarified.

The wicked gleam in his eyes said that if he thought she would allow it, he would kiss her again. The problem was, she knew she would. He crossed the distance between them and put his hands on her shoulders.

She tingled all over. Lower still, she felt a melting sensation.

"I know you think I'm a good guy—and I am."

Being alone with him always seemed like a dangerous proposition to her way-too-vulnerable heart. Especially now that they were legally married. Sharing space. Caring for their new dog. And expecting a baby…

Doing her best to maintain her composure, she inhaled a bolstering breath. "But…?"

He grimaced and dropped his hands, stepped back. "I'm also not a saint."

And they had promised each other this 120-day union of theirs would be in name only.

Trying not to fantasize about what it would be like if they both reneged on that, she pushed her romantic notions aside and forced herself to ask, "You're saying you don't think we could sleep side by side just for one night?" She gave him a long, measuring look. "Even if it is the most sensible way for us both to stay warm?"

* * *

Travis had no idea how to answer that. He knew what Skye wanted him to say. That it would be fine, and no inappropriate lines would be crossed. But the thought of her soft, warm figure snuggled beside his had his body in overdrive. And all he was doing was standing next to her, in the firelight, his palms still tingling from the mere act of cupping her shoulders. What would it be like if he gave in to impulse and kissed her again?

Would he be able to call himself a Texas gentleman then?

"I'm human," he said finally. Needing more space between them, he stepped back.

Skye looked hurt and confused. Which was the last thing he wanted, damn it all. "Meaning?" she asked in a low, trembling tone.

Aware there was something about being around her that made him want to throw caution to the wind, he forced himself to be brutally honest, for both their sakes. "It's no secret we have chemistry, darlin'."

Putting it in those terms made it a whole lot less romantic.

She blinked as if she wasn't sure she had heard him right. "You're saying...you'd want...?"

"I *do* want," he told her plainly, figuring the sooner she knew where they stood, the better.

With a gasp, she marched deliberately toward him. To his surprise, not stopping until they were mere inches apart.

"Well, that's the hell of it, cowboy," she murmured

back, her eyes growing all soft and misty. "I think I want, too."

Then, to his surprise, she rose on tiptoe and wreathed her arms around his shoulders. Her soft, sweet mouth moved up toward his. Instinctively, his lips slanted down.

The kiss was electric.

She moaned, responding with unabashed pleasure. Travis hadn't intended to let them get any closer than they already were. Hadn't planned to let the storm drive them into each other's arms—never mind the same bed for an entire night—because their situation was already complicated enough as it was.

She was vulnerable. So was he. And despite the fact they were now temporarily married and expecting a baby together, he did not want to take advantage.

But remaining emotionally distant from her, keeping things strictly platonic, was impossible when she melted against him like this, kissing him again and again and again. The blood thundered through him, heating and hardening his body. He reveled in her soft surrender, the raw need and fierce determination in her embrace.

They were both adults.

They had been in this situation before.

They knew what they wanted.

"You're sure?" he whispered, easing off her coat.

She pulled off her gloves. "*So* sure," she whispered back, looking up at him with a lusty smile.

Skye took him by the hand and led him into the next room, over by the bed, where a single lantern on the bedside table provided soft light. Lifting her arms to encircle his shoulders, she kissed him with a wildness beyond his most erotic dreams. Running her hands over his shoulders, chest, then deftly unbuttoning his shirt and stripping it and the thermal tee beneath off.

He did the same for her, removing her sweater and bra. Her breasts were fuller than he remembered, with pretty pouting nipples. He cupped their weight in his hands, running his thumbs over the silky globes. "So beautiful," he said.

"It's the pregnancy."

He smiled against her mouth. "Then I can't wait to see the rest of you…"

With her breasts pressed against his chest, her palms running up and down his spine, she rocked against him in a way that let him know that despite all the things they'd told themselves, a night like this was inevitable.

Drunk with pleasure, he finished undressing her and filled his hands with her soft, lush curves.

They kissed endlessly, until once again it was no longer enough. He let her undress him and call the shots, invite him into the bed and be in complete control. Until they were almost there. Then he laid her on her back and found his way to the feminine heart of her, helped her find the release she sought.

"Travis…" she moaned, arching, needing more. "Now… I want you now…"

He eased between her open thighs. Skye was trembling as he slid in, possessing her slowly, completely, then diving deep. She closed around him like a tight, hot sheath, and then they spiraled toward an erotic fulfillment more wondrous than anything he had ever felt.

Afterward, they clung together, still shuddering, breathing hard.

Travis eased up from the bed just long enough to add another log to the fire and grab the extra blankets. He brought them back and spread them out before climbing in next to her.

Smoothing the hair from her face, he studied her tenderly.

"I thought I imagined it before," she murmured wistfully, the picture of sated elegance in the soft lamplight. "How good it was."

The wind outside was counter to the cozy warmth beneath the covers. Travis traced the silky skin of her bare shoulder as they snuggled together.

She kissed his jaw. "What about you?" They shared another kiss, a deep one that let him know this could—*would*—happen again. "Did you imagine it would be like this?"

He stroked her hair and breathed in the citrusy scent of her shampoo, taking a moment to consider the question and answer honestly. "The part of me that likes life uncomplicated was certainly hoping that was the case," he said finally.

"And the rest of you?"

He exhaled in satisfaction, knowing it didn't get any better than right here, right now. "The rest of me... didn't realize how good a connection like that would feel." As if they were really and truly one.

She snuggled closer, sending his hormones into overdrive. "Do you think it's the baby?"

He hoped their situation would deepen the ties between them. But he wasn't experienced enough when it came to relationships to say that was what was going on. So he focused on what he *did* know. "I'm really excited about your—*our*—pregnancy."

"So am I." Abruptly, she went silent. He wasn't sure what she had been looking for in his response. He only knew she suddenly looked troubled. She rose up on her elbow, sliding a discreet distance away. "I want to see my ob-gyn and make sure everything is good before we tell anyone."

He understood. His sisters had felt the same way and hence delayed telling the entire family until the first trimester was over and they were sure all was well. "Agreed." Travis pulled her back into his arms, kissing her once more. "For now, it's our secret." And with that agreed upon, he made love to her all over again.

"You didn't have to do this," Skye said sleepily at nine the next morning, surprised to find how late she had slept. But then, she had been cradled in the cocoon of Travis's strong arms most of the night.

He handed her a plate of toast and eggs, plus a glass of juice, then gave her a lopsided grin, a sexy glint in his eyes. "It was no problem. Especially now that the power is back on."

The cabin was a lot warmer than it had been during the night, when they had recklessly made love and then cuddled together for warmth. Vaguely, she recalled the sound of everything starting up at once and the lights coming on. Travis's low voice in her ear, reassuring her, telling her to go back to sleep. Which she had. She smothered a yawn with the back of her hand. "That was about dawn, wasn't it?"

"Just before, yeah."

He'd told her to stay where she was while he got up to turn off the electric lights and put another log on the fire. She remembered snuggling deeper into the covers on the bed, drowsily falling back asleep. "Did you come back to bed?" she asked, ashamed to admit she couldn't quite recall. Although it seemed like he had...

Another indulgent smile. "Until Luna stirred at seven, yeah."

Skye sipped her juice. It was tart and sweet on her tongue. A glance out the window showed the sun was shining brightly. "How's the ice?"

"Melting quickly, I'm happy to report."

"Good to know." Unable to remember a time when she'd felt so cared for, she munched on her breakfast. It was every bit as delicious as it looked.

A man who can make love expertly? And *cook? I've clearly hit the lottery with this guy!*

"Yeah." Travis leaned toward her, his own mug of coffee in hand. "A couple of things—I talked to the HVAC company. They think they can send someone out later this afternoon to look at the ranch house furnace. Hopefully, they'll be able to get it up and running."

Skye had mixed feelings about that. She wanted the

furnace fixed, and she had come to love the big Victorian. Plus, she had a lot of happy memories there. More she wanted to build. But she would regret leaving the cozy dogtrot cabin, which was so rustic and charming, so very much...him. She flashed a grateful smile nevertheless. "That's great!"

Travis went down his mental list. "Also...my dad called. He could use an extra hand on the Circle L."

He seemed to be asking if she thought she would be all right without him. Which was sweet but unnecessary. She was pregnant, not incapable of caring for herself. She polished off her second piece of toast, waving off any concern. "Of course you should go."

"Third—my mom is hosting an impromptu cookie-making party for the grandkids at the same time to help ease their disappointment over not getting any snow they could play in."

Skye imagined the cheerful chaos. "That's nice of her."

"You're invited to attend, if you want."

Without him? After their surprise announcement the other day, followed by her fainting? Suddenly, it felt like a lot more than she could handle. "Um... I think I should stay here with Luna and work on contacting Realtors who specialize in ranch property—to see if any of them are interested and get their advice on whether we should try and do any more improvements to the property or just hold off for now."

He paused.

She had zero idea what he was thinking, never mind feeling.

"Makes sense," he said finally, in a carefully bland tone.

Heat gathered in her chest and spread to her face. Hastily, she added, "No disrespect meant, of course."

"None taken." A brief silence fell. The cozy postcoital euphoria faded even more, and he continued to study her as if trying to figure something out. "Anyway, if you're sure you will be okay staying here with just Luna, I'll be going."

Nodding, she went back to her breakfast. Though she knew it was delicious from previous bites, it now tasted like cardboard. She tossed him a breezy smile. "I'll be fine!" Then she watched him pull a fleece charcoal vest on over his flannel shirt and gather up his Stetson, gloves and suede shearling-lined tan coat. He was wearing his cowboy boots, too. She wished he didn't look so damn hot—even though he had yet to shower or shave—because it wasn't helping matters.

He put his cell phone in his vest pocket, zipped it shut. "Promise if you need anything, you'll call."

She loved the possessiveness in his low, rough voice. "I promise."

He came closer, inundating her with the masculine scent unique to him. "And you and Luna will stay here in the cabin and won't take any unnecessary chances until I get back."

Was he going overboard with the overprotectiveness? Maybe. Did she mind? Not one bit. "No slip and falls?" she teased, in an attempt to lighten the mood.

"Not a one, Skye," he said even more gruffly. He leaned forward to kiss her temple. "I mean it."

The sensation of his smooth, warm lips on her skin reminded her of their tender and fierce lovemaking the night before. The memory sent a hot, sexy sizzle all the way through her. She wondered how long it would be before they found their way into each other's arms again.

"I promise," she said.

Glad for the distraction from the wild turn his life had taken, Travis met his dad at the barn closest to the house and climbed into the passenger seat of the Circle L feed truck. Their task? Get food to the herd, then drive around looking for ailing newborn calves. "That was quite the announcement you and Skye made the other night," Robert said, driving slowly and carefully. The four-wheel drive truck crunched through the patches of ice and frozen slush.

Robert continued in the firm, loving, matter-of-fact voice of a man who had spent his entire life taking care of his family. His hands were scarred from a lifetime of hard physical work. "I mean, we knew you planned and hosted the memorial service for Walter and Willa together and had both resided at the ranch the last two years or so, but beyond that..." He squinted against the brilliant sun and reached for the sunglasses attached to the visor. "Your mother and I didn't even realize the two of you were dating."

Glad he'd already put his own sunglasses on, Travis murmured, "Ah. We weren't... Not exactly."

Robert nodded, still listening.

The silence in the truck grew, marred only by the crunch of the wheels over rough ice, slush and snow, and heavily crusted terrain.

When Travis offered nothing more, his dad said, "Is Skye...pregnant? Is that why she fainted? The reason for the speedy nuptials? You're doing the honorable thing?"

Ah, hell. He wasn't supposed to reveal this part of their situation just yet.

Yet he didn't want to lie to his dad.

He kept his eyes on the horizon, still looking for lost or hurt cows and calves. Finding none in distress yet.

Now that he was married, though, he figured his first allegiance had to be to his wife.

And Skye had made it clear: tell no one until after she had seen her obstetrician.

Releasing a gusty sigh, he said, "It's more complicated than you could even imagine, Dad."

They reached a group of one hundred or so cattle. Robert pushed the lever next to the console and released the feed. As it poured out of the truck and onto the ground, the cattle began to fall in line behind them, eating. "I've got time to listen," the older man said kindly.

Travis told him about the Braeloch will.

Another silence fell between them as they reached a gate. Travis climbed out of the cab and opened it. After his dad drove through, he closed the gate and climbed back in.

"So, you and Skye inherited equally?"

"Yeah, as long as we followed their last wishes and entered into a legal marriage for 120 days," Travis replied. "After that, we're free to split up, if we choose, and sell the property outright and share the proceeds."

"It shouldn't be hard to sell, if that's what you want," Robert said.

"We've already had an offer from a developer for two million dollars, but neither of us want to see the ranch be broken up. So we're probably going to hold out and find a family who can afford the place since they will have to pay more than that. Walter and Willa were clear—the property must go to the highest bidder."

Robert smiled. "I knew Walter and Willa were great businesspeople as well as ranchers. I also knew they were wildly in love. Their quiet affection for each other was legendary in these parts." He shook his head as if still trying to wrap his mind around the wacky situation Travis and Skye had found themselves in, courtesy of the Braelochs' matchmaking.

When they passed the herd, his dad cut off the feed lever once again. "So, you're saying this is just a marriage of convenience," he concluded stoically as they drove across the fields, toward another grouping of cattle. "Or is there more to it?"

It felt like more than that now.

But not wanting to be in the situation he'd been in before with Alicia—ending up a persona non grata—Travis exhaled. "We're just doing what was requested of us and taking it day by day in order to fulfill Walter and Willa's last wishes, Dad. Beyond that, I don't know what will happen—and at this point, neither does Skye."

"I can respect that." Robert slowed as they came up on a mama cow and a baby calf struggling unsuccessfully to stand.

Seeing the newborn was in distress, the older rancher stopped the truck and cut the ignition. Travis grabbed a blanket and the medical kit.

As they jumped out to render aid, Robert offered one last bit of parental advice: "Just make sure that you and Skye don't hurt each other in the process."

Chapter Eight

The HVAC repairman had just arrived and gone to look at the furnace in the Winding Creek ranch house when Travis pulled in. He emerged from his Silverado quad cab, his clothing covered with mud and other foul-smelling substances she wasn't sure she wanted to identify.

"I'd like to ask what in the world happened to you, but I fear I'd be repeating myself," Skye said dryly.

Travis shucked off his boots outside the door of the cabin, knelt to pet Luna and then followed Skye inside. He went straight to the laundry area to strip off his wet, grimy clothing.

Afterward, he strode nonchalantly into the bathroom and turned on the shower. It was all she could do to keep her eyes from devouring his gloriously naked body.

He flashed her an equally appreciative look; then, grinning, he stepped beneath the spray and began to lather up. Water from the overhead fixture sluiced over his muscular back, past his waist, to his sinewy buttocks and thighs. When she noticed again how smoking-hot he was, her mouth went dry.

Skye turned away from him, ignoring the low, insistent quiver in her belly.

Oblivious to the ardent nature of her thoughts, Travis finally said, "We found a couple of baby calves that were born in the storm or just after it ended. They weren't doing too well. We gathered them up. Their mamas took exception."

Skye lingered outside the open bathroom door. She shut her eyes, willing away temptation as she worked to slow her racing pulse. "I can imagine." She swallowed around the sudden dryness in her throat, then looked at him again, asking curiously, "Where are the newborn calves now?"

He rinsed the shampoo from his hair. "In the barns. And you'll be happy to know the baby calves have been reunited with their mamas." Finished, he reached for a towel and dried himself off. "Tess Gardner, the new large-animal vet who is working with Sara Anderson-McCabe, was on her way over when I left, but I imagine all three calves will be fine with some additional nutrition."

She moved away from the doorway, giving him a wide berth. He smelled incredibly good, like the brisk ocean-scented soap he favored. "Is that why your dad wanted you to go over and help out?"

Travis slipped on boxer briefs and a clean T-shirt. "That, and he wanted to talk to me."

Uh-oh. This does not sound good.

"What about?"

Travis put on a clean flannel shirt, thick wool socks and jeans with the same swift efficiency he'd used to strip down. "Our announcement Thanksgiving evening."

"What did you tell him?"

"That we were just honoring Walter and Willa's last wishes."

Put like that, it sounded…quite unromantic.

Which, of course, was what it was *supposed* to be.

She let out a strangled sound of indignation. "Don't you think we should have discussed it first?" She was irritated they hadn't. After all, they had come to terms about their pregnancy announcement, in advance. Why not this, too, for heaven's sake?

Travis rubbed a towel through his hair, unperturbed. "Probably, yeah. But since my dad was asking a lot of questions—and Griff is going to file the will with the probate court in Laramie County on Monday morning—the news is going to go public soon, anyway. I just preferred my mom and dad hear it from me directly first."

Okay. This just went from bad to worse. "You told *Carol*, too?"

Travis sat down to put on a pair of boots. "Briefly, before I left," he affirmed, his attitude as pragmatic as usual, when it came to matters of the heart. "We didn't talk long, since I was a filthy mess and she had the cookie-baking marathon with the grandkids going on inside. But she got the basics."

Skye wasn't sure whether to be relieved or anxious about the way it had all unfolded. "How did she take it?" she asked warily.

The sexy lips she loved kissing took on a downward slant. "Honestly?" Shrugging his broad shoulders, he said, "I think she was disappointed. She's always wanted all eight of her kids to have the kind of bigger-than-life romance she and Dad have."

The minute the words were out of his mouth, Travis knew they were a mistake. Just as he could now see that telling his dad—without clearing it with Skye first—had been wrong.

Before he could correct either, Luna let out a short bark, and there was a knock at the door. The HVAC repairman was on the porch. He was grinning from ear to ear. "Good news! It's fixed," he said.

Smiling, Skye went to stand next to Travis, her pique with him temporarily forgotten. She had the debit card they had been given for ranch expenses in her hand. "That was fast," she said to the repairman.

"Turned out to be a faulty thermostat." He showed them the bill. It was reasonable, and they both nodded their approval. He slid the debit card into the reader attached to his tablet. "I put a new one in. You're good to go. The heater's on now. Although, be warned—it's an old unit that's not particularly efficient, and it was about fifty degrees in the house, so it's going to take a few hours to really warm up."

They thanked him. He said to call if they had any further problems, then left.

Travis and Skye faced each other. "You want to stay here tonight?" he asked.

And just like that, the tension was back in her slender frame. She released a breath and looked down at her hands. "Actually...since I have to work tomorrow...and I've got some laundry to do before that, I think we should go back to the ranch house now. Or," she amended hastily, meeting his eyes once again, "at least *I* should, if you and Luna want to stay here, where it's warmer..."

Is this the way it's going to be? he wondered in frustration. He'd displeased her once. Made a misstep. And she'd put him in the deep freeze? He'd expected better than that. Reverting to the same coolly aloof manner, he asked, "What would you prefer?"

"Honestly, it's your choice." Something inscrutable came and went in her dark brown eyes. "But as long as we are on the subject of what should be taken care of next, Luna hasn't had any real exercise since yesterday morning."

He had the feeling that while all that was true, she also wanted her space.

Suddenly, he needed his, too. He shoved his hands into his pockets. "I can walk her."

"You wouldn't mind?"

He cupped her shoulders so she wouldn't bolt and looked down at her. "She's *our* dog, Skye. And no, I'd be happy to help Luna have some fun and get some fresh air."

Skye breathed an obvious sigh of relief as she gently eased away. "Okay, then…"

And just like that, they were back where they had started the morning before. Sharing space and married, it seemed, in name only.

Skye knew she was running hot and cold with Travis. But she couldn't help it. What he had inadvertently blurted out about his parents wanting him to have some huge romantic love had been way too reminiscent of her ex and his family.

Dex's parents had accepted her, of course, when there had been a baby on the way, and their social status in the community to consider. The Stones always did the honorable thing.

But the minute she'd lost the baby, it was all over. They'd wanted so much more for their son—and Dex wanted more, too. More freedom, more time to focus on his career, more years of dating a variety of women.

He was still single, she'd last heard. Still merrily playing the field. Without an heir in sight.

As Travis would be, had they not reached out to each other in profound grief and accidentally gotten pregnant. Their joint inheritance and the terms of the will had complicated matters even more.

As had the storm.

The hours spent sheltering inside his cozy cabin had cast a romantic glow over their situation. But things were back to normal now—or as normal as they would be for a while. She had to remember that.

"Something sure smells good in here," Travis said when he and Luna came in the back door of the ranch house an hour later. He headed straight to the sink to wash his hands.

"Chicken and dumplings." Skye had needed comfort food. He might need it, too, when he heard what she had to discuss with him.

He lifted the lid off the pot on the stove, breathed in the simmering stew. "Nice."

She took in his ruddy cheeks and windblown hair, the masculine grace with which he moved. "It's ready now, if you are."

He seemed to pick up on her cautious, overly bright tone. "Sure…"

He set out food for Luna, then helped Skye bring everything to the round 1950s diner-style table in the kitchen, which had been with Walter and Willa for most of their married life. It had a chrome frame, as did the chairs. The Formica tabletop was a sunny yellow, as were the plush padded vinyl backs and comfy seat cushions of the chairs.

The set didn't quite go with the sage green of the repainted cabinets, although it did coordinate nicely with the new hardware Willa had chosen for all the pulls and the new stainless steel appliances. But the large country kitchen was still a work in progress. Needing new countertops and backsplash. Missing the big island with extended seating and additional prep space Willa had longed for.

Treating this more like a business meeting than the cozy meal for two that Walter and Willa had probably envisioned for them, Skye sat opposite him and said, "You know I have been contacting ranch Realtors yesterday and today."

Nodding, Travis spread his napkin across his lap.

Skye helped herself to some salad. "Well, I heard back from someone," she announced as she poured poppy seed dressing on top. "Her name is Cristal Ricci. She's located in Houston."

Travis followed her lead, though he skipped the dressing altogether. "You say that like you have reservations."

Because I do! Skye dug into her salad. "She wants to come out to preview the property early Monday afternoon."

Travis lifted a brow. "She knows we don't intend to put the land on the market until spring, right?"

"Yes, but…" She took a sip of ice water, quenching her suddenly dry throat. "Cristal still wants to see it *now*."

"And you object because…?"

"The kitchen isn't fully updated yet. And a family that can pay upwards of two million is going to want an efficient, modern kitchen. So I'm just not sure it's a good idea to show the property yet without renovating first."

Finished with the salad, Travis added a hefty portion of chicken and dumplings to his plate. "And yet you seem to be considering it."

Their fingers brushed as he passed the serving bowl

to her. She added a smaller amount to her dinner plate, then continued conversationally as they ate, "To really fulfill Walter and Willa's final wishes so you and I can move forward, we have to find a family who wants to bring the property back to its glory days. Given how little interest I've had thus far, that may not be such an easy proposition."

"It's only been a day and a half since you started notifying ranch Realtors of our intent. And it *is* a holiday weekend. Plus, there was one heck of a storm. With power outages in our area of the state."

"True." She took a bite and savored the rich, nutrient-packed stew.

"But…?"

"Usually, if salespeople are interested in acquiring your business, they waste no time getting back to you, even if it is just to set up a time to talk." She frowned. "And thus far, Cristal Ricci is the *only one* who's done that."

Another shrug, this one even more diffident. He picked up his glass. Sipped. "So maybe we should forget about what everyone else hasn't done…yet. Take that as a good sign and see what this Cristal Ricci person has to say."

"Fair warning…" Skye didn't know *why* she was so anxious, just that she was. "I've only texted and emailed with her so far, and she is really pushy."

Broad shoulders flexing beneath the soft fabric of his shirt, he sat back in his chair. "I can handle that," he assured her. "And so can you." He paused for another breath-stealing moment, his expression growing even more inscrutable. "But if you want to tell her you can't do anything until after the holidays—or even late spring— then I'm okay with that, too," he said.

Once again, Travis noted, he had said the exact wrong thing. Did Skye want him to be difficult to deal with, too? To somehow get worked up to go toe-to-toe with this Houston Realtor neither of them had yet met? Because that definitely wasn't his style.

Skye cut him off with a shake of her golden brown hair. "I don't think we should tick her off from the get-go—especially because for all we know, she already has a buyer or buyers in mind."

He finished his plate and helped himself to more of the delicious home-cooked entrée. "So, you'll show her around on Monday?"

"I really wanted you to be here, too."

Travis pulled out his phone and accessed the calendar. "I'm supposed to put up an outdoor holiday display for a client in town."

"Can you reschedule?"

Travis sighed. He wasn't sure why, since they had known this marriage was a short-lived proposition from the start, but he really didn't want to be part of developing an exit strategy. Especially now, when they were just getting used to the idea of having a baby and a parental connection that would last a lifetime, regardless how the rest of their relationship went. He sought the right words, but they didn't come. "You really need me here?"

Her pleading gaze did him in. "I want us to walk through this process together."

That sounded better. More like the family they were eventually going to need to be when the baby got here and permanently entwined their lives. Plus, she was right: Walter and Willa had stipulated in their will that they make all the financial decisions as one. "Okay. I'll contact them."

Her relief palpable, Skye began to clean up. He joined her.

When they had finished, she said, "I'm working the seven-to-seven shift tomorrow, so I have to be at the hospital by six a.m. Which means I have to get up by five and leave here by five thirty at the latest."

What was she trying to tell him? Something, it seemed, besides her actual schedule.

"So—" she made a big show of yawning and rubbing her eyes "—I'm probably going to read awhile and then turn in really early."

"Alone." He hadn't intended to say the word out loud. But now that he had...

She nodded.

She was probably right, he thought. They each did need their own space. Last night had been spectacular— but they had also been trapped in a cozy cabin in the midst of a winter storm. With an abundance of adrenaline and sexual energy.

Now they were back to normal.

Participants in a 120-day marriage that had not been their idea.

"Luna can sleep in my bedroom tonight, if you like. And I can feed her and take her out before I leave."

Unlike her, he did not have to work tomorrow. Plus, the dog was their responsibility, just as the baby would be. "I can handle that."

She gave him a brief assessing glance. "You're sure?"

"Positive," he said.

"Okay, thanks." She flashed him a quick friendly smile; then she knelt to say good-night to Luna, turned and went up the staircase.

And just like that, they were back to being roommates who barely interacted—except for the required one shared meal a day and sleeping under the same roof every night.

He tried not to feel too disappointed.

On the other hand, shouldn't he have seen this coming? At the end of the day, this was a business transaction, and that was all.

Chapter Nine

"Hope the storm didn't impact your honeymoon too much," Ashley, one of Skye's fellow nurses in the CCU, teased the following morning.

"Well, you know what they say…" Ron winked as he headed for the breakfast buffet the hospital cafeteria provided. "Nothing like a little adversity to help you get to know your spouse."

Happy she'd had the foresight to notify her coworkers of her elopement, the day before, so they would have time to get used to the change in her marital status, Skye bypassed the staff-room coffee and helped herself to some calcium-infused orange juice instead. Then she sat down at the conference table, watching as everyone else came in for the change-of-shift report.

Happy her coworkers were taking the news so

well, she smiled and said, "We had that, all right."
She launched into the story of how they had rescued
Luna and now were fostering and hoping to permanently adopt her. Then she told them the tale of woe
about their malfunctioning furnace and the necessary
move to the cabin.

"Sounds hectic and cozy." Hailey grinned.

It was, Skye thought wistfully. Especially when
compared to the lonely night that had followed, where
it had been back to separate bedrooms. She got out a
pen and the pocket notebook she carried with her. "So,
what happened last night? How were the patients?"

Everyone sobered.

Another day began.

Skye was so busy working, she had little time to
think about her personal life, never mind talk about it.
Twelve hours later, she clocked out, grabbed her coat
and bag, and headed out, eager to go home and see Luna.
And Travis, too?

As her heart skipped a beat, she had to admit that
was the case.

She had just emerged from the employee entrance
when she saw Travis's youngest sister, Emma, coming up the walk. The footwear designer had a gift bag
and Get Well Soon balloon in hand.

"Hey there!" The woman paused to give Skye a brief
familial hug, which Skye returned.

Skye stepped back. "On your way to see someone?"

"Yes. One of my friends just had surgery. She's pretty
bummed, so I figured I'd come by to cheer her up." She

switched the balloon and gift bag to her other hand. "You're just getting off work, I guess?"

"I am."

"Then I won't keep you long." Emma flushed, suddenly looking a little embarrassed as well as very determined. "Listen… I already talked to Travis about this when I saw him this afternoon, but… I realized later that I never actually said congratulations after you and Travis made your announcement over Thanksgiving."

So that's what was bothering Emma—she thought she had been rude or unwelcoming. "That's okay." Skye smiled. "It was a little chaotic." Especially after she had fainted. And plenty of other family members had said congrats.

The other woman sagged in relief. "Travis was right, then. He said you weren't upset about that. Which, I guess, under the circumstances… I mean, the whole reason why you apparently got together…" Her voice trailed off lamely.

Skye blinked in shock. "He told you about the will, too?"

Emma nodded, serious now. They stepped to the side of the cement walk to allow other visitors going into the hospital to move past. "I mean, the inheritance aside, it's a pretty noble thing to do—personally sacrificing months of your life to chase after someone else's unfulfilled dream of having a happy family with kids living at Winding Creek."

That was certainly a romantic way to look at it!

"To be honest, I was surprised," Emma babbled on nervously. "Because one, Travis has never liked taking orders from anyone. And two, Travis has never cared about material things. In fact, he's the complete opposite."

Was she fishing for information? Trying to figure out where Skye stood on the whole inheritance thing? Deciding she may as well be blunt, if Travis hadn't been already, Skye said, "I wouldn't mind having a financial safety net, just so I would never have to worry about ending up destitute if I were ever to get sick—" *or have a baby and want to take unpaid maternity leave* "—and be unable to work for a time."

Emma studied her with something akin to admiration. "He said you are really practical."

The way the other woman spoke, it seemed like everything Travis had said was highly complimentary. Skye couldn't help but be happy about that. She wanted Travis to like and respect her as much as she liked and respected him. Even if she would have preferred he cleared these kinds of revealing familial conversations with her first. But maybe that wasn't the way it worked in a big happy family like the Lockharts. "Sounds like you talked a lot about me," she said casually.

"Well… I was curious after Mom and Dad spread the word about the 'required' aspect of your nuptials in regard to the Braeloch will. Even though Travis is a lot older than me, I still wanted to make sure he knew what he was doing…" Emma paused for the first time since they had started speaking, obviously at a loss for words.

"Is there something you want to ask?"

The shoe designer nodded. "What's the endgame here? One hundred and twenty days married? Then you sell the property to a family who intends to ranch and go your separate ways?"

"Yes."

Emma frowned. "I know it sounds simple now—"

"But you don't think it really is?"

Emma leaned forward, confiding, "Tom and I initially got together last spring for noble reasons, too. All we were going to do was help each other out for a set period of time. And then, when things calmed down, we were going to return to our normal, very separate lives."

Their love story, like the rest of the Lockharts' love stories, was one for the ages. "Only you fell in love and got married instead."

"Yes."

"That kind of hyperromantic result is not going to happen here." Even though part of her very much wished it would.

"Maybe not with you," Emma agreed with something like relief. "But when it comes to matters of the heart, Travis is a lot more vulnerable than he would ever let on. Our parents' death and his long time in foster care left him very wary. The only time he ever let his guard down was when he was with Alicia. When it became clear she had just been using him to help renovate the house they were sharing, he pretty much told me he was *never* going to get involved with a woman for all the wrong reasons again. Probably never get married, either."

Skye shut her eyes briefly and rubbed the tense muscles in her temple. "Except he and I did. And while it wasn't what either of us wanted, we're kind of stuck as we try to do the right thing."

Emma nodded, mulling that over. "I can see that. Speaking of the right thing… You should know…even when he makes a misstep, as we all sometimes do, Travis's heart is *always* in the right place. So…" She paused meaningfully. "Try not to be too hard on him."

Her mysterious warning given, Travis's sister hurried on through the hospital's main entrance.

What in the heck does that *mean?* Skye wondered.

It had almost sounded like Emma knew something she didn't.

But she had no clue what it could be.

When she got back to Winding Creek, though, and saw what was on the front porch of the ranch house, she realized what her sister-in-law had likely been talking about.

Travis had thought bringing home a big beautiful Christmas tree and a pretty evergreen wreath would at least win him a smile. Instead, Skye was staring at both as if they were kryptonite.

He and Luna walked down the front porch steps to greet her. However, when he tried to relieve her of the belongings in her hands, she held on tight. *Okay.* She didn't want him to be gallant. Or give her a welcome-home hug, apparently. He stepped back slightly to give her more space. "Long day at the hospital?"

She crouched to greet Luna, whose black, brown and white tail was still wagging madly. Her smile seemed reserved for their canine pal.

"The usual." Brow furrowed, she rose gracefully. "Did we talk about putting up a wreath and tree for the holidays?"

Definitely not pleased. "No, but I figured we would decorate."

Still glaring at the tree, she went back to holding her insulated lunch bag and tote in front of her like a protective shield. "You usually don't, though, do you?"

No question, that was accusatory. Like he had done something wrong. He accompanied her up the steps, retorting mildly, "Not in the dogtrot cabin. But then, I don't really need to, since I go to my folks' ranch and married siblings' homes for all the actual holiday celebrations." He peered at her closely before opening the front door and ushering them in ahead of him. "But you helped Walter and Willa decorate here, didn't you?" He had been called on to pick up and bring in a tree, get it in a stand for them; but that had always been it. They'd been able to handle the rest themselves. And they hadn't bothered with any outdoor lights or decorations.

"Yes, I did." Skye set her things down on the foyer table, then went back outside to examine his purchases. She still did not look happy. Not at all.

He followed her, as did Luna, whose tail was no longer wagging. Instead, the pooch looked as upset as he felt. "Did you want something bigger?" Travis asked finally.

Skye blinked. "Than *that*?"

It was nearly seven feet tall. "Smaller?" he tried again.

She waved off his inquiry, turning away brusquely. "It's fine." She marched back in the house.

"You don't look as if it's fine. Did you want to drag the prelit artificial one that Willa and Walter used to put up, years ago, before you came to work for them, out of the attic?" Because he had put that one up for them as well, and carried the boxes of ornaments down from the third-floor attic.

Obviously, she had seen it. Skye removed her coat and scarf and hung up both, then regarded him with escalating exasperation. "I think that one had its day many moons ago."

She had a point.

Skye walked in to the living room, then looked around even more critically. She was in one hell of a mood. Which, from what he understood, could be the norm for pregnant women due to all the hormones and stuff. Even so, it was nice to have her home again, with him and Luna. The big Victorian was lonesome without her.

He cautiously edged closer. "Then what is it?"

She plopped down on the very middle of the sofa, giving him a choice: squeeze in on either end beside her or take the chair opposite her. He settled in the wing chair.

She glared at him. "Cristal Ricci is coming to the ranch at noon tomorrow, Travis."

He nodded; she had texted him the time earlier when the arrangements were set up. "Exactly. Everyone in my family told me today when we all went to the lot to pick out our trees together that if you are going to sell a place during the holidays, or even trying to generate interest, you need to decorate it."

Skye went very still, looking only slightly less peeved. "Did Emma agree with this advice?"

Luna jumped up on the sofa and settled beside Skye, then put her head in her lap, offering what comfort she could.

Trying not to smile at their affectionate little companion, Travis kept his mind on the issue at hand: his buying a tree as his first holiday surprise for her. "Ah. Actually, no."

Some of the steam went out of Skye as she stroked Luna's long silky ears. She bit her lip. "Why not?"

Figuring what the hell—if Luna could cuddle with Skye, he could, too—Travis moved over to sit on his wife's other side. He shifted to give her a little more room and to better see her face, he draped his arm along the back of the sofa. "She thought I should wait and pick out a tree with you."

Skye turned slightly to look at him, too. "You disagreed," she guessed.

Aware she was starting to appear slightly more conciliatory, Travis stated calmly, "I didn't think it mattered as long as we decorated it in a way that was mutually pleasing to both of us."

She let out a long, slow breath, still looking a little troubled. "You're right."

"Except I keep feeling I'm not right, darlin'."

Skye gave Luna one final pat on the head, then stood and began to pace. "It would have been silly for you

not to pick up a tree when you were already there with
your family."

Which means, what? Travis wondered. He stood,
too, leaving Luna still curled up on the sofa, then strode
nearer, still searching Skye's pretty upturned face.

He paused, finally starting to get what was wrong.
"Did you want us to do that together?"

For a long moment, Travis's question hung in the
air between them.

*Did I really want us to do that particular chore
together?* Skye wondered. Common sense said she
shouldn't care—but deep down, she did. It hurt that
she had been shut out of this pivotal moment, their first
holiday together. Especially after all the Christmases
she had spent after her parents, and then her aunt, died,
without any family to call her own.

Yes, kindhearted strangers had taken her in, invited
her to their family dinners. And during the two years
she had been with Walter and Willa, they had included
her in their festivities as well.

But now they were gone, too. And she had steeled
herself to spend another holiday without family. At
least, she had until she'd married Travis in name only
and been welcomed by the Lockhart clan.

So, right or wrong, she had assumed she would have
a family again this Christmas, even if only by virtue
of her 120-day marriage.

Only to find out that was a misconception, too.

Without warning, her eyes filled with tears. She
turned away. To her horror, a sob rose in her throat.

She tried to stifle it with her fist. Too late, because Travis knew she was upset. The next thing she knew, she was in his arms, crying about so many things. The baby she had lost before. The baby she was going to have now. The marriage that should have been simple but was not.

She cried about her fear over the future.

Her worry this pregnancy might end badly, too.

The idea that she and Travis might end up hurting each other, and if they did that, then they'd hurt their unborn infant, too.

"Hey," he said softly, stroking her hair and holding her close. "It's going to be okay. I promise. I'll... I'll donate the tree, and we will go and get another one together."

The idea was so ludicrous, it made her giggle. "Don't be silly." She sniffed, shaking her head at her own idiocy. "We don't need to do that."

He tipped her face up to his, forcing her to look at him. "Then what do we need to do to make you feel better?" he asked her with a gentleness that touched her very soul.

And suddenly, she knew. Skye released a long, slow breath and surged against him. "This..."

Understanding exactly what she wanted, Travis tunneled his free hand through her hair and slowly, deliberately brought his lips to hers. The pressure of his lips and the plundering sweep of his tongue made her heart soar. She only wanted one thing: to be even closer to him. She wreathed her arms around his strong, broad shoulders, melting against him in liquid pleasure. And still, he kissed her as if he meant to make her his.

Completely caught up in the moment, she arched against him, smoothing her hands down the warm, solid muscles of his back. She moaned again, loving the hard, masculine feel of his body cradling hers. Never before had she been so tempted to just take each moment as it came, without thought or worry over the future.

"Upstairs?" he growled against her mouth, as if feeling the same driving urgency.

"My bed," she replied, knowing there was only one man, one cure for the quivering need deep inside her.

"Your wish is my command." Without warning, he scooped her up in his arms and cradled her against his chest. Still kissing her, he made his way through the first floor, up the stairs and down the hall to her bedroom. He set her down next to the bed. Just that easily, her scrubs came off. Undies followed. Her nipples pearled as he regarded her ardently, sexy purpose glittering in his eyes. And then he was on his knees, his face pressed into her lower midriff.

Skye shivered as his thumbs traced the most intimate part of her while his lips took a sensual tour of her bare stomach, lingering over her navel, drifting lower still. A slow warmth began to fill her. She closed her eyes, lifting herself to him, aware she was way ahead of him.

She groaned. "I had something more mutual in mind," she said, unable to stop the soft, sultry sound she made in the back of her throat when he kissed and touched her again.

"Hush," he teased. "I'm busy here…"

Skye let out a trembling laugh while he caressed

her again, demonstrating just who was in charge, until yearning welled up inside her, until she was his for the taking.

Her whole body turning hot and boneless, she guided him to his feet. And then his clothes were coming off, too, and it was his turn to release a low, shuddering moan. He took her in his arms again, and kissed her deep and hard, long and slow, his tongue hot and wet and unbearably evocative. Her hands glided over him; his magnificent chest, his abundant sex—all hers to enjoy. Joy bubbled up. Passion built. She fisted her hands in his hair, urging him on. It all felt so good. *He* felt so good. And she whimpered at the pleasurable ache swirling deep inside.

He emitted a low sound of triumph, then delivered another deep and searing kiss, cupping the soft swells of her breasts in his palms, loving her again with his mouth and his lips and his hands.

Needing that blissful peace only he could give, she urged him down onto the bed. He rolled over to kiss her, still fueling and fulfilling her desires with shocking ease. His hands went to her hips, and she arched against him. And still, they kissed, finding each other with their hands and their lips and their tongues, willing each other not to stop until she was writhing with passion and moaning for more, and he was hard and hot.

"I want you inside me when I come," she whispered, then gasped again, moving against him wildly. Already teetering on the edge, she wasn't sure she could take much more.

Her hands slid beneath him, her hair drifted over his

spread thighs. Ardently, she urged him on. Loving his response. He groaned. "I want to be inside you, too."

He tightened his hands on her, urging her upward. His hard body surrounded her with masculine warmth, giving her a whole-body shiver. He kissed her again, long and lingering, and she surrendered completely, opening herself up to him as she wrapped her arms and legs around him. More kisses followed, and then he slid home. That's when the real magic happened. They made love to each other as partners in pleasure, as if nothing else in the world mattered. And for that brief moment in time, nothing else did.

Afterward, Travis held her close, stroking her hair. "I still don't know why you were crying." He kissed her temple, then her ear. "And if I don't know why, I can't fix it."

Skye sighed and rested her head on his shoulder, loving the solid masculine warmth of him. The way he went all out to protect her, even when it wasn't necessary. She ran a hand over the bunched muscles of his chest. "It's not up to you to fix my tears. I'm pregnant." *And I'm a newlywed in a very unexpected situation.* "Which means I'm overly emotional."

He rolled so he could see her face. As their eyes locked, she couldn't help but think how right it felt to be with him, especially like this—when there was nothing between them but the yearning to be together, as one. "It has nothing to do with me disappointing you?" he asked gruffly.

She had the feeling he was comparing her to his ex. The knowledge that even though he had given Alicia his all, it had not been enough in the end. Just as what she had offered Dex had not been enough. Skye didn't want to go down that same path any more than Travis did.

Which meant she couldn't blame him for her own issues. She had to face it: life had given her plenty of baggage long before he'd ever entered her life. It was her responsibility to get rid of it, own up to her idiosyncrasies. Not his.

"Nothing at all, I swear," she told him honestly. It had to do with all the things she was no longer able to control or predict; her ongoing adjustment to life in a big loving family who sometimes got all up in each other's business; as well as her fear over the uncertainty of the future. And Skye knew only time would fix that.

"I think you ate more than I did," Travis remarked an hour later, glad he'd thought to provide dinner even though he'd had no idea if she would be hungry when she got home from her twelve-hour hospital shift.

Skye snuggled next to him on the sofa, looking cute and comfy in flannel red-plaid pajamas, a long red cardigan and slippers. She dabbed at the corners of her mouth. "That's because I'm eating for two now."

He returned her teasing glance, surprised how good it felt to be doing even the most mundane things with his new wife. "Hmm." He nodded at the baking sheet that held the New York-style pepperoni pizza he'd picked up shortly before she got home and since re-heated for them. "You want this last piece?"

Skye winked at him. "It's all yours, cowboy."

"Mmm. Generous. Except I'm stuffed, too."

She sobered. Gratitude tilted the corners of her lips. "Thanks for providing our evening meal."

"It just seemed like a pizza night." He studied her freshly scrubbed face and brushed hair. A companionable silence fell. Funny how out of sync they could sometimes feel with each other until they made love. Then they were both on the same page, wanting intimacy and satisfaction and closeness. The overwhelming kind he only felt when he was with her. Wrapping his arm around her slender shoulders, he drew her into the curve of his body. "You feeling better now?"

"Yeah." Skye released a contented sigh, still snuggling close. "The lovemaking helped."

So they *were* on the same page—at least with this. Travis stroked his palm down her arm. "That's an admission I didn't expect."

"Me either." She pinned him with a sidelong glance. "But why pretend we don't want each other?"

Travis had figured this acknowledgment would come eventually; he just hadn't expected it this soon. Happy it had, though, he shifted her onto his lap. "Can we also stop pretending we don't want to actually sleep in the same bed?" Because the night before had been lonely as hell after the bliss of spending hours wrapped in each other's arms.

She searched his face. "You really want to sleep with me?"

Skye seemed unsure that would be the case. He understood why. In some ways, sharing a bed for an entire night was more intimate than sex. More gratifying, too. "I do," he told her quietly. "Every night."

She studied him, then warned, "That could blur the lines even further."

He chuckled. "Do you hear me complaining?" he chided her gently. "Besides, the lines have already been blurred by the baby."

"True."

"So do you really think we should waste time trying to set limits every which way we turn when we could simply enjoy being together over the holiday and share the excitement we're both feeling about the baby?"

With a soft laugh and a shake of her head, she relented. "No…"

Hallelujah! It is *the season for miracles!* "So is that a yes to sleeping together every night?" he pushed on. "And making love whenever it works for both of us?" Which he hoped would be most of the time.

"Yes." She grinned. "And speaking of our baby…" She settled more comfortably on his lap. "My first OB appointment is scheduled for Wednesday at four p.m. We should be able to hear the heartbeat…" She paused, hope lighting her eyes. "You said you wanted to go…"

"Darlin', I wouldn't miss it for the world." For this, and every other aspect of their pregnancy, he was all in.

Chapter Ten

Travis stood next to Skye on the front porch of the ranch house at noon on Monday, watching the powder blue Mercedes convertible coupe come speeding up the lane. They'd had a call a few minutes before letting them know that Realtor Cristal Ricci was about to arrive. And, not knowing how she felt about dogs, they had decided to leave Luna inside when they came outside to greet her. He squinted as the coupe approached the house. "It looks like she has someone with her."

Skye shrugged and bit her lower lip. She had been antsy all morning, pointlessly tidying up and moving things around. But then, maybe this was how people always acted before a showing. "An assistant, maybe?" she guessed.

They already knew this particular big-city Realtor

was pushy, to say the least. But it meant a lot to Skye to go ahead and test the market for the property, which was why he was going along with it. A positive review would help her relax; a negative one would give them a lot to work on before spring, when they actually listed the ranch.

A win either way.

Except...

"That's no underling," Travis murmured as the two women stepped out of the car and onto the drive.

The blonde driver was already approaching them, her hand outstretched. All business, she was dressed in a sophisticated pantsuit and heels. "I'm Cristal Ricci." She tilted her head toward the statuesque brunette beside her, who was wearing a silk dress and an abundance of very expensive jewelry, and carrying herself with the air of old Texas money.

Which was, Travis knew, the last kind of person who Willa and Walter would want taking over their beloved Winding Creek Ranch. No matter how much she was willing to pay.

"I brought a client along to preview the property, too," Cristal continued brightly. "This is Izzie Wheaton."

He greeted their guests with the grace he'd been raised to exhibit. "I'm Travis Lockhart," he said as they shook hands. "And this is my wife," he said, unable to help feeling a little bit proud to call her that, even if it was a temporary prearranged situation, "Skye McPherson."

Smiling, Skye put her hand forward, too. "Nice to meet you both."

Izzie Wheaton was already looking around, one elegantly shaped brow raised. "It's certainly...rustic."

Which, as it happened, was the nicest thing she said over the next hour and a half while they toured the inside of the ranch house and the dogtrot cabin, as well as the stable, barn and outbuilding that now served as Travis's workshop. A trip around the two-thousand-acre property via Travis's pickup completed the viewing.

"Where are the cattle and horses?" Izzie asked.

Travis held on to what little was left of his patience. And it wasn't much. "We don't have any."

"But it's already set up for both," Cristal pointed out helpfully, "so they could always be added."

Izzie contemplated this. "Well, that makes the smell better in the meantime, I guess. Which is a plus since I don't know how 'country' my husband and kids are likely to feel when they first arrive to see the place."

Indeed.

Travis couldn't imagine this woman wanting to live on a working cattle or horse ranch. Skye didn't look all that hopeful, either. He braced himself for the inevitable rejection.

Izzie turned to Cristal and sniffed in disdain. "Okay, well, in any event, I want it," she said.

Skye knew this was a disaster from the moment the two women had arrived. She should have waited to contact other Realtors instead of letting the anxiety over the future get the better of her.

Izzie turned back to Skye and Travis. "How soon

can the two of you be out?" she demanded. "Because I really need to get my interior designer and contractors in and get this place ready for the holidays. And, as you can imagine, that is going to take *a lot* of doing."

Skye figured she had gotten them into this quandary; she should get them out. "Even if we wanted to sell now—and we don't, not until April, as we told you when we first emailed with Cristal—it would take weeks, if not months, to get everything finalized."

"Not if the buyer waives all inspection and pays cash," Cristal pointed out matter-of-factly, stepping in to broker a solution. "Then the deal could close in a day."

"I know because I've done it," Izzie said confidently.

Skye was sure she had.

"And I'm going to need the time," the woman continued, "if I want to get at least fifty cattle and horses for Kirk and the kids here in time for Christmas. As well as a couple of hired hands to care for the animals."

She was speaking as if it were all a done deal.

Travis held his ground as surely as Skye held hers. "If that's the timetable you want, you should keep looking," he said affably.

"I agree," Skye said, stepping closer to him. Although she didn't need the protection, in a situation like this, she still enjoyed leaning on his strength.

Izzie frowned at her phone, then at them, before plastering on a persuasive smile. "Look, if you're worried about getting all your stuff packed up and out, I'll pay for that. Even put it in storage, if you want."

Her eyes narrowed when she saw they weren't

budging. "I'll even foot the bill for a hotel while you look for another place," Izzie added.

Skye had never liked being pushed around. A look at Travis's face told her he felt the same.

"Not happening," he said.

Izzie blew out a furious breath. She glared at both Travis and Skye. "Handle it," she told the Realtor, and headed for the coupe, cell phone in hand.

Cristal turned to them. Desperate. "I don't think you-all understand," she whispered. "Izzie is the sole heiress to *Wheaton Oil*. When she wants something, she gets it. And she wants to buy her husband and kids a ranch and surprise them with it at Christmas."

And who said money couldn't buy happiness? "There must be something else available for her," Skye said.

Cristal removed the sunglasses from the top of her head and waved them around. "This time of year? No one puts property on the market between Thanksgiving and Christmas."

For good reason, Skye thought.

"Plus," Cristal continued, "she wants something similar to what Kirk's great-grandfather owned in west Texas when Kirk was a kid. And this is apparently it."

That was an emotional reason, if misguided. But Skye and Travis had feelings at stake here, too. "Then why can't she buy that?" Skye asked.

"Because it's a subdivision now."

Just like Winding Creek could one day be.

Cristal cast a wary look over her shoulder and tried again, warning, "I've known Izzie for years. She's not going to stop until she gets what she wants."

Travis and Skye exchanged glances. They were in perfect agreement.

"Well, she is *not* going to get this," Travis said.

"Did that just happen?" Skye watched the Mercedes speed off, still feeling a little shocked by the events of the afternoon.

Looking handsome as ever in a flannel navy-plaid shirt, down vest and jeans, Travis inclined his head. His whiskey-colored eyes sparkled ruefully. "Seems so."

Unwilling to admit just how much she wanted to spend time with him, Skye observed, "You don't seem surprised."

He shrugged. "You never know what someone has going on behind the scenes. People with that much money often feel a lot of pressure to keep up with the Joneses."

Skye paused in surprise. He spoke as if from experience. "You've seen that kind of behavior before?"

"Yes. My brother Cade was a professional baseball player. When he got his first pitching contract, it was a lot of money. He got all sorts of advice about where to put his earnings, to maximize his investment so he'd have a hefty nest egg left when he finally retired. Plus, for the first time in his life, he could literally walk into any place, no matter how ritzy, and buy whatever he wanted on the spot. He also felt the pressure to have several fancy cars—like all the members of his team— live in a very luxurious mansion and so on."

Skye found that hard to imagine. "Cade seems so

down-to-earth now." At least, he had when she met him at Thanksgiving.

Travis nodded. "Part of that is due to his wife, Allison. She and Cade keep each other grounded and focused on what's important."

The two had seemed close—as did the rest of his married siblings with their spouses, Skye couldn't help but note a little enviously.

"Believe me," Travis continued, "if Cade hadn't come back to the values he grew up with, she never would have gotten back together with him and married him."

He spoke about it so passionately. Which made her wonder: "Do you still have those values?"

His lips compressing in acknowledgment, Travis took her hand in his. "Probably to the other extreme. But yeah. I honor the *people* in my life, not the things."

Something else to admire about him.

Still holding on to her hand, he studied the downward curve of her lips. "You still upset about Izzie Wheaton's plan to have us out in a couple of days?"

He was right. That had rankled her. Skye lifted her chin, indignant. "Who asks anyone to vacate their home a few weeks before Christmas, for any reason?"

"I know, right?"

Skye turned to look around at the view, which was spectacular, with the rolling hills, tidy pastures and the tree-lined banks of the creek that wound its way through the property. She'd sat on the wraparound front porch of the ranch house many an evening with Walter and Willa, relaxing and enjoying the spectacular sunsets. "It's the thought of having one last Christmas here that has kept me going the past few months." She had needed time and space to really absorb her loss. Because the Braelochs had been the only family she'd had since losing her own. And now they were gone, too.

Travis turned to look at the undecorated pine tree they had put up near the window in the living room, the wreath that had made it on the front door. He squeezed her fingers, and tingles spread throughout her entire body.

"Walter and Willa really loved Christmas," he ruminated sentimentally.

Feeling somehow unbearably restless, Skye disengaged their hands and paced to the far end of the porch railing.

After swallowing, she said, "I wanted to honor their memory by celebrating it here one last time."

He came closer. "Then we better get cracking on it." The warm affection in his eyes deepened. "Since Christmas will be here before we know it."

"How did work go?" Skye asked when they sat down to eat their brisket sandwiches and coleslaw several hours later. He'd gone into town to finish a job, and in his absence, she'd picked up some new lights and a few ornaments for the tree to add to the others.

To her delight, he'd brought home takeout from Sonny's Barbecue, and they'd opted to take their plates into the living room and sit on the sofa.

Skye had lit the fire before Travis got in. He smiled down at Luna, who was sitting quietly at his knee, hoping for a taste of brisket. "Great." He rewarded their new pet with a small bite. Tail wagging, Luna gulped it down. Travis sat back against the cushions and continued chowing down on his dinner. "Mrs. Davidson is always so appreciative of anything I do for her."

Unable to help but note how ruggedly handsome he looked with his windblown hair and ruddy cheeks, Skye asked, "What was it today?"

Travis polished off one half of his sandwich and went to work on his slaw. "Putting new weather stripping on all her windows and doors."

Skye savored the delicious meat and soft, warm bread. "How did you get into handyman work, anyway?"

He added a little more barbecue sauce to his meat. "I worked my way through Texas Tech at a home-repair service." He replaced the top of the sandwich half and paused to take another bite.

Skye sipped her decaf iced tea. "Sounds like a good job. Practical and engaging."

"It was. Although the learning curve could sometimes feel steep," he admitted ruefully, "since I was just out of high school."

"I can imagine." They exchanged smiles.

Finished, Travis put his plate aside. "Anyway, I mostly apprenticed on two-person jobs for the first couple of years."

She tried to imagine him at that age and came up with independent to a fault, kind and generous. Loving the intimacy of these evenings together—maybe the Braelochs had been onto something with this one-meal-a-day-together-every-day idea—she smiled at him once more. "How did that go?"

"Good. The senior technicians were always patient with me, explaining everything I needed to know to do each particular task properly. By the time I graduated, I was a senior tech, teaching other young kids."

Signaling for him to stay put, Skye took their plates in the kitchen and returned with the treats she'd picked up while in town—white chocolate-peppermint brownies from the Sugar Love Bakery.

"Thanks," he murmured as she handed him his.

Their dessert was decadent and delicious. Skye was happy to note he seemed to be savoring it as much as she was. Aware she could so get used to hanging out with him like this, she forced her mind back to the conversation. "Did you enjoy helping others learn the trade?"

"Yeah." Once he was done eating, he rose and gathered up the dessert dishes. He carried them into the kitchen, then went to get the brand-new boxes of tree lights.

"So what did you major in when you were in college?" Skye asked.

Travis opened up the end and began unwinding the strand of lights from the cardboard insert. "Agriculture business and cattle management."

She held the end while he continued to unravel. "Did you like that?"

"Yeah." He wrapped the lights around the very top of the tree.

She moved to accommodate him, doing her best

to stay out of his way. Nevertheless, their bodies still brushed up against each other occasionally. Tingling, she stepped back, unraveled the strand even more. "Did you ever work as a rancher?"

Travis towered over her, expertly threading the lights through the branches. "Mmm-hmm." He smelled like peppermint and soap and the brisk winter wind. "For the first year or so, after I graduated, I worked on my dad's ranch." He bent down to do the middle of the evergreen. "He wanted me to take over the Circle L when he eventually retired."

Skye went to get another box. She opened it up. They fused the lights together, and Travis continued wrapping while she assisted. "That didn't work out?"

He kept his gaze on his task, guarded now. "It did and it didn't."

Which means what, exactly? she wondered. "What was good about it?" she pressed, really wanting to know.

He turned to her, his gaze sifting over her face and lingering on her lips before returning to capture her eyes. "The physicality of the work. Being outdoors all day. Caring for animals, seeing they get what they need."

His jeans stretched across the taut muscles of his thighs as he hunkered down to finish stringing lights across the bottom of the fragrant evergreen.

"And what *wasn't* so great?"

When he was done, he stood. "I was the boss's son, tapped to one day run the ranch, who really hadn't earned his place on the Circle L." Frustration turned the corners of his lips down. "The other hired hands were fine taking orders from me, but it never escaped any of us that they had years of experience on me and knew a hell of a lot more." Finished with that strand, they went to get the rest of the items Skye had purchased. "Luckily for me, they were all good guys and were as generous with their knowledge as the senior techs at the home-repair service had been."

She watched with satisfaction as he pulled out the star and put it on the top of the tree. "So why did you leave?" she asked as they stood back in tandem to admire it.

Travis reached for the new strands of cranberry-colored garlands. They wrapped the tree with those, too. "I realized it was going to be at least twenty years before my dad retired. Although he liked having me with him, he didn't really need me. And I wanted something of my own, that I built from the ground up, even if it was a heck of a lot smaller enterprise."

As he neared her, she breathed in the tantalizing scent of his hair and skin. "How did your dad take it when you told him?"

Travis exhaled, his broad shoulders flexing beneath the soft flannel of his shirt. "He was really disappointed." His eyes crinkled in regret. "Of all eight of his kids, I was the last hope to take over the ranch. But he understood my need to be my own man and offered to gift me some acreage from the Circle L to get started with my own ranch."

The heat emanating from his tall, strong body brought forth memories of their lovemaking, creating a hollowed-out feeling in her middle. "Did you take it?" She looked into his eyes, happy he was confiding in her this way.

"No." He reached over to brush a strand of hair from her cheek and tenderly tuck it behind her ear. With a soft smile, he let his hand drop. "I wanted to do it all on my own. But I needed capital for that. So I started a handyman service to bring in extra cash, fast. Willa and Walter were among my first customers. They rented me the cabin. As part of our deal, I kept the pastures mowed, the fence repaired—and in return, they let me clean out one of their barns and use it as a workshop to do things like repair window screens, sand down and paint kitchen cabinet doors, and so on." He cleared his throat. "Meanwhile, the handyman work was booming. I always have a waiting list that goes at least a month out, and I really enjoy working with people."

She could see that, and loved the way his face lit up when he was talking about his work. "So you've given up on the idea of having your own ranch and raising cattle or horses?"

He paused. "I had."

She sensed there was more. "Until...?"

He stood, legs braced apart, arms folded in front of him. He leveled his serious gaze on hers. "We found out we were having a baby, and I realized how important it is for a child to have a permanent home they can count on."

Chapter Eleven

Travis noted that this was apparently not welcome news to Skye. "You're considering going back to ranching now?" she asked.

"Not exactly. Not full-time."

She stared at him in confusion. "Then…?"

"I spoke with Griff yesterday while you were at work, about how binding the terms of the will were. He said once we fulfill the marriage contract and inherit the ranch as a married couple, it will be ours, free and clear. And then legally, we can do as we please."

Travis knew he was taking a lot of license here; but with a baby on the way, everything had changed. And he felt sure that if Walter and Willa were still here, they would understand that. He also knew how Skye longed for a financial safety net. The kind that meant she would never, ever have to worry again. He was re-solved to provide that, too.

He moved closer, drinking in the feminine citrusy scent of her hair and skin. "What I'm trying to tell you is that we don't have to sell Winding Creek, Skye. At least, not the ranch house and cabin and barns and the sur-rounding one hundred or so acres. We could just sell off the majority of the land and put the cash we would gain from that in trusts—one for you and one for the baby."

The tension in her shoulders eased slightly. "What about you?"

That was easy. "My share is going to go to you and the baby."

"That's not fair to you and not really what Walter and Willa wanted, either." Her voice grew as troubled as her expression. "They already regretted having to sell off over five hundred acres the last twenty years to continue living on the ranch after they'd retired and stopped running cattle."

Travis exhaled. "I know each acre they lost was painful to them." Empathetically, he continued, "Since they had no children and they'd spent all their lives building and expanding this ranch, this land was their legacy."

"Exactly. They wanted what was left of the property to stay in one piece and go to a loving family with kids, who would bring it back to life…"

Travis nodded. "A loving family like us…who just happen to be having a baby right now."

He was certain Walter and Willa would prioritize the family they were fast becoming over land.

She threw up her hands in frustration. "And in theory, that's great, Travis. But in reality, we can't afford to stay here long-term right now on our own. Us selling the ranch piecemeal wasn't what Walter and Willa wanted, and we know it. So whether we have the legal right to do it anyway isn't the point."

Ouch!

"The ranch isn't set up now to run cattle and/or horses," she went on, getting more fired up with every second that passed. "And, most important of all, I'll be having our baby mere months from now, and I want to take maternity leave for at least six months, which is unpaid. I don't have enough savings right now to support that." Her lower lip trembled. "Which means I'd have to go back to work a lot sooner than I'd like…"

Travis reached out to tenderly stroke her cheek. "No, you won't. I can support you and the baby, Skye. Especially if we continue to live here and I figure out a way to start running enough cattle to pay all the ranch expenses. My other income can pay the rest."

She frowned at him. "It's not your responsibility, Travis."

"You're having our child, so… I think it is."

She opened her mouth to speak, then shut it again, rubbing at the crease in the center of her forehead, as if that would keep a sudden headache at bay.

He hadn't meant to upset her.

And she was right: it was really too soon for them to be talking about this. Although he knew what *he* wanted—and he would move heaven and earth to financially support his wife and child, and give them the happy, secure life they both deserved.

Instead, all he had done right now was muck things up. "I'm sorry." He dropped his hand to her shoulder. Waited until she finally lifted her head to look him in the eye. "We have a plan."

She looked so fragile in that moment his heart ached for her. "We do," she said.

"So we'll stick to that now," he promised. *Or at least until we have a better one that she likes more...*

"Now, where were we?" he asked, turning back to the boxes of ornaments he had brought down from the attic.

She studied him, her heart suddenly on her sleeve. "I was thinking we should use these first." Skye opened up the lid of the plastic storage box. "As a way of commemorating Walter and Willa. And then add the new ones I bought today."

He held her gaze. "Sounds good."

She handed him two glass ornaments, plain red-and-gold balls, and took more of the same for herself. For a few minutes, they hung them in thoughtful silence.

Wanting to see her beautiful smile again, he pulled out his phone and selected Christmas music he had downloaded. He hit Play. The happy sound of Ed Sheeran and Elton John's "Merry Christmas" filled the room.

She turned in surprise. "Oh, I love that song!"

"Me too." He hooked his arm around her waist and drew her close. He leaned down, cupping his free hand around his mouth, and pressed it against her tummy. "And Baby needs to get in the spirit of the season, too. Right, little one?"

Her melodious laugh filled the room. "I don't think he or she can hear you yet," she teased.

Travis winked, straightening to his full height. "You never know."

Skye drew in a tremulous breath. "I am excited."

He paused to kiss her softly. "Same here."

She drew back, sweet affection in her gaze. Knowing if he kissed her again right now they would never get the tree finished, he went back to the ornaments. There were two tissue-wrapped ones nestled at the very bottom. He took one and handed the other to her.

"Oh!" She stared at the sterling-silver wedding bells, which had Willa's and Walter's names and wedding date inscribed across the front. "This was the only thing they could afford to give each other, aside from the tree, that first year they were married." And it had been on their tree every year since.

He opened his. It was a sterling-silver heart with the date of their seventieth wedding anniversary on it. "And this was the last ornament they ever bought," he recalled gruffly.

Travis turned to see Skye wiping away tears as she hung the ornament on the tree. Feeling his own eyes well, he folded her into his arms. She laid her head on his chest. "Oh, Travis," she sniffled. "I miss them so much."

"I know, darlin'." He stroked her hair and held her close, breathing in the sweet womanly scent of her.

Savoring her femininity and her warmth. "I miss them, too," he told her. Doing his best to be strong for her, he soothed, "We were lucky to have the time we did with them."

She drew back to look at him, the tears sliding unchecked down her pretty face. "You're right. And I know they will always be in our hearts."

"Yes, they will be." He paused as the next realization hit. "Which is maybe why we were gifted with this baby... To help us heal and focus on the future Walter and Willa wanted for us."

Skye hadn't expected to be doing this again so soon, but as they kissed their way to her bedroom, she couldn't help but think about the closeness she felt whenever they were together. What was one more blissful interlude than something to be grateful for? And despite her lingering grief, she was still appreciative of so much. And right now, in this moment, her gratitude was focused on Travis, the feel of his strong arms around her as he disrobed her and then himself before stretching out on the bed beside her.

A delectably sweet kiss followed. They rolled onto their sides, facing each other. She pressed the softness of her breasts against the solid warmth of his chest.

And still, they kissed and stroked and caressed each other as sensations ran riot inside her. He was making her feel not just wanted but *needed*—and cherished, too.

Easing a thigh between hers, he stroked her slowly, erotically, moving her closer to the brink. Unable to help herself, she made a low sound of surrender in her throat. He smiled against her mouth and continued to lay claim to her the way only he could. Touching and kissing her breasts, caressing her tender nipples, patiently moving lower, making her moan even more deliriously this time. He found her sensitive spot with the pad of his thumb, continued stroking, then laved it with his lips and tongue. She shuddered with the headiest sensations she had ever felt; and then she was catapulting into bliss. Coming slowly back.

He moved upward, sliding his hands beneath her, lifting her. "You like this?" he murmured.

"Yes!" she whispered back, opening her legs to him, trembling with sweet anticipation.

Then he slid home with one smooth stroke. And there was no more taking it slow. No more holding back. Only hot, sultry kisses and searing possession. Unimaginable pleasure and exquisite release.

They came back to Earth slowly. Skye lay with her head nestled in the curve of his shoulder, her body still cozily entwined with his. He shifted the hair away from her face and bent to kiss her again, softly and tenderly. Then, with a reluctant sigh, he eased his weight off her. Rolling onto his back, he kissed the top of her head and tucked her against him.

She rested her head on his chest and draped her arm and leg across his hard, warm body. He chuckled affectionately. "Every time, I think it can't possibly be as good as I remember," he confessed, "and then it's even better."

She laughed softly, too, still savoring his warmth

and his strength as he lovingly stroked his hand through her hair. "Exactly what I was thinking…"

He held her eyes. Emotion shimmered between them. There seemed like there was a lot more he wanted to say as the barriers between them began to re-erect. But when he finally spoke, it was of the mundane. "I need to get dressed, turn off the tree lights, bank the fire and take Luna out one more time," he said.

She struggled not to yawn, feeling guilty for not thinking of all that. They were supposed to be in a true partnership here, at least for the next few months. She started to get up, too. "Hold on, cowboy. I could do some of that—"

"No. You and Baby stay put." He spoke to her tummy. "Hear that, little one? It's nighty night time."

More laughter bubbled up. Skye loved his silliness. It was a side of him she had never imagined seeing.

"Seriously," she tried again. "I need to do my part." This time, she could not stifle a yawn.

Travis looked down at her lovingly. He caressed her cheek with the pad of his thumb. "Don't you have to work tomorrow?"

"It's Tuesday, so yeah."

Reluctantly, he began pulling on his briefs and jeans. "Is your schedule the same every week?"

Skye nodded. "I have twelve-hour shifts on Sunday, Tuesday and Thursday, and every other Friday. Seven in the morning to seven at night."

"And you set your alarm for five?"

Which reminded her—her cell phone was downstairs on the charger. So she reached over and set the alarm clock next to her bed. "Yep." She lay back against the pillows, suddenly feeling exhausted. "Forgive me if I fall asleep before you get back?"

His hand stilled, and he stopped buttoning his shirt. For a moment he looked hurt; then he resumed dressing, casual as ever. "Of course not." He cleared his throat. "Good night, then."

With a brief smile, he turned and headed out. She heard him whistling for Luna as he made his way down the stairs.

Obviously, he'd thought she had been politely dismissing him and asking him to leave.

Which was sort of true. And sort of not.

The romantic side of her wanted more cuddle time and pillow talk. Another lovemaking session. Yet the other, more realistic half of her knew she was already getting way too involved. The fact they were married and living as a couple, combined with the magic of Christmas and the baby on the way, had her conjuring up completely unrealistic dreams. But those dreams were not the way her future was likely to go. *I have to remember that*, she thought as she drifted off to sleep.

Chapter Twelve

Travis and Luna got up to see Skye off the next day, giving her the best start to the morning ever!

Unfortunately, their schedules did not mesh well over the next twenty-four hours. She had to stay an extra few hours after her shift at the hospital to help out with the admission of a new critically ill patient, and was so exhausted when she got home on Tuesday evening, she fell straight into bed.

Travis joined her, snuggling her close—until their blissful sleep was interrupted by a call at four o'clock Wednesday morning from a regular client. They'd had a flood in their kitchen when the intake valve in the dishwasher broke, and they had woken up to the sound of rushing water. They wanted to know if Travis could intervene before any more damage was done.

He said sure and took off, but not before telling Skye where he was headed and promising to meet her at the ob-gyn's office for their appointment later that afternoon.

As it turned out, she arrived twenty minutes early. He was already in the parking lot, sitting in his truck. Seeing her, he emerged and strode purposefully toward her. The dark wool sweater he wore brought out the whiskey color of his eyes. His tailored slacks did equally nice things for his lower half. She let her gaze drift all the way down to his polished boots before returning to his face. "You look nice."

"Thanks." He smiled down at her. "I grabbed some clean clothes before I left this morning. Cade and Allison let me shower at their place."

Which, Skye knew, was located in the heart of Laramie, a few blocks away.

His siblings were always there for each other; it was part of the Lockhart family credo. "That was nice."

He returned her smile with an easy one of his own. "It was." Then his gaze drifted over her cranberry knit dress and matching jacket, lingering on the suede ankle boots made by his sister Emma. He leaned over to give her brow a quick kiss. Letting his hand rest on her waist, he regarded her appreciatively.

Moments later, they fell into step beside each other. She slanted him a look. "Did your client's crisis get resolved this morning?" she asked curiously.

"Yeah. I'm glad I went, though. The hazmat team wasn't able to get there until around eight, and a lot more damage would have occurred if we hadn't been able to work together to mitigate it."

"I'm sure they were glad to have you come to their rescue." She sure would have been!

His grin admitted this was so. Together, they continued threading their way through the packed parking lot and toward the building. "I went to the appointments I already had set up for today after that."

"Busy times," she murmured. Another wave of the butterflies she'd been experiencing all day engulfed her middle.

He assessed her with a sidelong glance, then wrapped a steadying arm around her shoulders. "You okay?"

She leaned into his strong, reassuring touch, imagining how wonderfully tender and protective he was going to be with their child, too. Then, as the residual anxiety that had been dogging her all morning came to the fore once again, she asserted just as softly, "Mmm-hmm." She prayed for it to be true.

Travis caught her hand as they moved through the glass doors of the medical building. The lobby was momentarily deserted, so he moved her against the wall and then looked her in the eye, as always seeing far more than she would have wished. "Tell me," he insisted in the gruffly commanding tough-yet-tender tone she loved.

Their gazes intersected. Suddenly, her emotions came tumbling out in a nervous rush. "Well, I know—" She stopped and corrected herself, "I mean, I *think* everything's perfectly fine. But…" She gulped, blinking back hot, embarrassed tears. "I have been pregnant once before, and that ended in a miscarriage…" What would happen if she suffered a similar loss?

Travis had learned enough from his mom and four sisters to know the biggest mistake he could make in a situation like this was to either discount Skye's fears or pretend to be able to see the future.

It didn't matter what he thought and hoped would happen. Only what his wife was feeling right now.

Her rare show of nerves breaking his heart, he wrapped his arms around her and held her close. "Whatever happens today, just know that we're in this together."

She nodded, her face pressed into his shoulder. Finally, her trembling eased and she drew back. Her face was still pale, but the fear in her eyes had been replaced by her customary resolve to conquer whatever life difficulties came her way.

She squeezed his hand and held on tight. "My doctor's office is on the second floor."

Still holding hands, they took the elevator up, walked into the office and signed in. They were able to sit side by side while Skye filled out the necessary paperwork. Twenty minutes later, they were in the exam room. She had on a pink cloth gown and a sheet across her lap. Travis was happy to be at her side. Happy to be included in all this.

Dr. Johnson came in, along with a nurse. He was kind and exceedingly thorough as he went over her medical history since her last physical. Travis stood at her shoulders and held her hand while she put her feet in the stirrups, and a physical exam was done. Afterward, the obstetrician turned back to them and said, "You said you think the conception was on August twentieth?"

"Um, actually we know it was." Skye blushed.

He checked the data on the computer screen in front of him. "That means you have a due date of May 13." Then he got out the fetal Doppler and ran the handheld device over her middle, stopping when a *thump-thump-thump* filled the air. "That's it?" Skye asked in excitement.

Dr. Johnson nodded. "Your baby's heartbeat. Nice and strong."

Travis thought he had known pure joy before that moment. And he had, whenever he was with Skye. But sharing this moment with her took it to a whole other level.

The baby's heart continued beating, loud and strong.

Skye's eyes were filled with tears.

His were, too.

"Everything is looking good." With satisfaction, the doctor turned off the fetal Doppler. He settled in front of the computer where he was making his notes. "What questions can I answer for the two of you today?"

Skye inhaled shakily. "What are the chances I will have another miscarriage?"

Travis wanted to know that, too.

"Statistically," Dr. Johnson informed them both

gently, "miscarriage is usually a one-time occurrence. Less than one percent of women have another."

Wanting to be there for Skye as much as she needed him to be, Travis clasped her trembling hand in his. Held tight.

"Additionally," the ob-gyn continued, "you are now past the first trimester, when most occur. So, as I said, everything is looking great with this pregnancy."

Hearing that, Skye smiled in relief. She looked up at Travis, gratitude shining in her eyes.

"Will you do an ultrasound?" he asked.

Dr. Johnson typed in a few notes on the chart. "At the five-month mark," he affirmed. "Unless there is a problem earlier, which I am not anticipating."

As the moment drew out, Travis noted that Skye still seemed a little worried. Phrasing his words carefully, he asked, "What can we do to ensure the baby has the best start possible?"

"You can take these every day." Dr. Johnson handed Skye a few samples and prescriptions for prenatal vitamins and a folic acid supplement, plus a glossy information folder that said Your Pregnancy across the front. "In addition, get plenty of rest, eat sensibly, limit caffeine and exercise as you would normally. And avoid stress as much as possible."

That was all doable, Travis thought.

"And, of course, call the office if you have any questions or concerns. Otherwise, I will see you in one month," the physician said. "But before you go—an encore." The obstetrician ran the fetal Doppler over

Skye's tummy one more time. Grins abounded as the now-familiar *thump-thump-thump* filled the room.

"That was really nice of Dr. Johnson to give us a second listen to our baby's heartbeat," Skye remarked as they left the office.

"I've got to admit," Travis said, taking her hand as they exited the doctor's office and walked out into the main hall, toward the elevators, "it was reassuring to hear such a strong and healthy heartbeat from our little one."

Skye leaned into his tender grasp, wishing she had both arms free so she could really hug him. She didn't because the samples and information packet wouldn't fit into the small handbag she had brought with her. "Very much so," she agreed emotionally.

As they turned to face each other, he gently kissed her lips.

The elevator dinged.

His sister Faith swept out, heading straight for the ob-gyn's office, too—until she saw the two of them, that is. She stopped dead in her tracks, shock turning to delight. "Hey! Fancy meeting you-all here!" she said. "Although it appears I may have interrupted something?" she teased, referencing their sweet kiss. Then her eyes fell to the items in Skye's hands.

Skye blushed.

The three of them stood there half a minute longer, chatting awkwardly; then Faith, who was late for an appointment of her own, rushed off.

Skye waited until they had reached the privacy of

the parking lot, her previous excitement replaced by a welter of uncertainty and embarrassment.

"What's wrong?" Travis asked, guiding her over to stand next to his pickup.

Sighing, Skye turned her face up to the gray skies, letting the chill of the December day wash over her. Her dreams of keeping things simple and easy seemed even further away. She was used to having complete privacy in her personal life—one of the few perks of being without family to call your own. No one butted in or passed the latest happenings along to everyone else.

Now, in addition to the entire Lockhart family knowing about the real reason behind their marriage and the inheritance, there was this, too.

Still holding the pamphlet and prenatal samples, Skye told Travis anxiously,"Your sister knows about our pregnancy."

Travis shrugged. "So what if she *did* figure it out. We're having a baby, Skye! On or around May 13! And we heard his or her heartbeat today. And soon, we'll be feeling him or her kick!"

His enthusiasm was contagious. She took comfort in all Dr. Johnson had told them and imagined all Travis had just laid out. It *was* pretty fantastic. Despite her wildly veering emotions, she broke out into a grin. "Excited much?" she teased.

"Hell yes, darlin'!" He picked her up by the waist and swung her around, not setting her down until she was fully wrapped in the cage of his strong arms.

He kissed her, and she kissed him in return, reveling in the hot, male taste of him. The way he could make her forget everything but him and the moment they were in. The way he made her believe she was everything he had ever wanted—when she knew he was fast becoming the same for her.

When the lip-lock finally ended, he stepped back and said, "How about dinner?"

To Travis's satisfaction, Skye agreed a celebration was in order and thought that the Tex-Mex restaurant Mi Amigos was the perfect venue.

"Feliz Navidad" was playing when they walked in, adding to their joyful mood.

The waitress led them to a leather-backed booth in the middle of the restaurant. She handed them menus, then returned with a bowl of hot, crispy tortilla chips and fresh-made salsa. By the time she returned with their drinks, they'd had enough time to look at the menu and knew what they wanted. They placed their orders, then sat back to wait.

Skye couldn't stop smiling, he noted. And neither could he. "So, what do you think?" he asked, letting his admiring gaze sift over her. She looked so pretty in that cranberry dress, her golden brown hair flowing over her shoulders in soft, tousled waves. "Do you think we're going to have a girl or a boy?"

Her eyes sparkled as much as her smile. "No clue."

Loving the way she acted when she got excited about something, he asked, "Should we find out beforehand?"

She released an enervating breath that lifted the soft, enticing swell of her breasts. "Maybe wait and be surprised, is what I'm thinking now—but if you ask me two months from now, when we're going in for the ultrasound, I may have an entirely different answer." Her grin morphed into a satisfied smile. "What do you think we should do?"

In an effort to get comfortable in a booth that was slightly too small for his large frame, he shifted his legs beneath the table, briefly bumping knees with her. Tingling from the accidental brush of their legs, he drew back, then took her hand, softly conceding, "Whatever you want to do."

"That's not an answer, cowboy."

He inclined his head, trying not to notice how right it felt to be here with her like this. As if they were on a date. The kind they should have had plenty of before saying "I do" and making love. "It kind of is."

She lifted a brow.

"Haven't you heard the saying 'If Momma ain't happy, nobody's happy'?"

"I have." Skye sobered. "But I don't intend to be like that. I want this to be an equal opportunity parenting adventure."

"Me too."

For a long moment, they held hands across the table, looking into each other's eyes.

He wanted to take her to bed so bad.

He also wanted to get to know her so much better than he did. And the way to do that was by asking questions. Reluctantly, he let go of her hands. Sat back as they both sipped their drinks. "Do you have any major wishes when it comes to bringing up our baby?" he asked.

"Our baby," she whispered back.

Damn, he liked the sound of that.

She moved her shoulders eloquently, obviously thinking something yet seeming reluctant to reveal it. Which was just like her. Quiet and shy to the core—in her personal relationships, anyway.

He tried again. "When you imagined having a family of your own one day, where did you see yourself living?" he asked as they casually began to eat the crisp, salty chips dipped in Mi Amigos's famous tomatillo salsa.

Still watching him dreamily, Skye rested her chin on her upraised fist, confiding quietly, "Well, I always thought I would end up back in the country at some point—in a rural area like Laramie. But not in town."

When he raised his brow, she clarified, "I saw myself on a little plot of land somewhere. With room for a garden and a dog, and a big swing set or play fort for the kids."

Her eyes darkened, and she regarded him, intrigued. "What did *you* imagine?"

"I didn't. Not really. I mean, the assumption that I would marry one day and have a family of my own was there—from my parents and all my siblings, who have all been or are married and have kids themselves now."

"But you couldn't visualize it?" She leaned back as their dinners—a steaming plate of enchiladas for her, sizzling fajitas for him—were put in front of them.

Travis picked up his fork. "It's kind of a hard thing to do if there's not a specific woman involved you want to spend the rest of your life with, who is also thinking the same way. And up until now, there hasn't been."

She cut into the corn tortilla covered in ranchero sauce and watched the melted cheese ooze out. "Alicia?"

"Didn't want marriage or kids. So, in the end," Travis said as he opened up a flour tortilla and built a fajita for himself, "even if she had been interested in taking our relationship to the next level, it probably never would have worked."

"So." Skye sat back and sipped her lemon water. "Are you saying that's changed?"

"Yes. I am." The moment drew out, and he admitted gruffly, "Our marriage may have started out in a very unexpected way, but now that we're living together and we have a baby on the way... Well, I can finally envision what everyone in my family has always wanted for me. A white picket fence and all the trimmings."

"That's good." She ducked her head shyly.

Not about to let any misconception pass, he leaned across the table to kiss her, softly and sweetly. "And if I'm being honest, Skye, when I think of my future now, the first thing I think about is you."

Travis's words stayed with Skye through the rest of the meal, their individual drives back to the ranch, and through the feeding and walking of Luna before bed. And she was still mulling over his words when they made love later and fell asleep, wrapped in each other's arms.

Too soon, though, her alarm went off, and she had to get up for work.

As before, Travis got up, too, and fixed breakfast for her. "Call me if you need anything," he said. "Anything at all. No matter how small and insignificant it may seem."

If this was how he was reacting now, how would he behave when her due date was upon them? "How about I call you, but only in an emergency?" she teased.

He gave her a mock salute as he walked her to her car. "Just know I am here for you, darlin'. Ready, willing and able. Whenever you need me."

Everyone was in a cheerfully merry mood at the hospital when she arrived for morning report, too.

"Well, if it isn't our resident lovebird," Ron drawled as Skye took her place at the conference table.

Ashley chuckled. "You're right. She does have that special newlywed glow…"

"Well, at least we know now we don't have to worry about them. It is a real love match." Hailey grinned.

Skye rolled her eyes in exasperation, opened up her yogurt and sprinkled some granola on top. "What are you-all going on about?" she asked, miming their playful tone.

Ron, who was happily married himself with a couple of teenage kids, chuckled in approval. "Last night. At Mi Amigos?"

Skye paused, the spoon halfway to her lips. Oh dear. What had they heard? "What about it?" she asked cautiously.

"My wife and I were there, too."

And she'd been doing what she never did in public: participate in PDA! "Oh. I'm sorry." Did they think she had dissed them on purpose? Flushing hotly, she sat back in her swivel chair, met her coworker's eyes. "I didn't see you."

Ron unwrapped his breakfast sandwich. "Or Carol and Robert Lockhart, either, obviously."

Skye felt her appetite fade altogether. "My new in-laws were there?" she asked, mortified.

"Yeah. Apparently, when they walked in, they started to go over to your table to say hello, but then you and Travis got all googly-eyed and started holding hands and making out—"

With a huff, she corrected, "We *weren't* 'making out'!"

Ron disagreed. "Well, it was one hell of a kiss…"

Skye buried her face in her hands. "Ohmygod…" She looked up. "What was Carol and Robert's reaction?"

Ron took a bite of his egg-and-sausage biscuit and closed one eye, thinking. "If I had to characterize it, I would say they were pleased and approving. And not willing to interrupt what was obviously a very private and romantic dinner. So they had the waitress sit them where they couldn't see your table and you couldn't see them."

Skye covered her face with her hands once more, wishing she could sink through the floor and disappear completely. "Why didn't you say something?"

He took a sip of his coffee. "I was going to, but by the time my wife and I had finished our meal, you two had already left in a rush."

"We had to get home to take care of Luna, our new rescue dog."

"Uh-huh." Hailey, a new bride herself, giggled. "*Likely* story..."

Luckily for Skye, the night nurses came in at that moment to update them on everything that had happened during the shift. Talk quickly turned to their patients, and the shift change that followed left no room for any more joshing about her romantic life.

The quandary she and Travis were in stayed with her, however. She texted him when she took her morning break. Need to talk with you ASAP. Can you stop by when I take my lunch break?

Be right there, he immediately texted back.

It's not that urgent, she typed back.

And got nothing in return.

Fifteen minutes later, when he strode in, she was just about to return to work. But Ron looked at Travis's concerned expression and reached out and touched her arm. "I'll cover for you," he offered. "Go ahead and take your lunch hour now."

"Thanks."

Skye took Travis by the elbow and steered him into the nearby supply closet, shutting the door behind them.

"Well, I guess I could get used to this..." he drawled with a salacious wink, having apparently figured out this was not a medical emergency having to do with their baby.

She waved off the joke, too tense to indulge in repartee. "I just found out your parents were at Mi Amigos last night at the same time we were."

He sobered immediately. "How?"

"My coworker Ron—whom you just met—and his

wife were there, too!" Skye wrung her hands together. "Apparently, everyone there saw us making out!"

Travis looked at her like he could have cared less. "That's sort of what happens when you share a kiss in public, darlin'."

"Don't you get it? Your family is going to figure out we're expecting." She stabbed a finger against the middle of his chest. "That is, if they haven't already."

"How?"

Ohmyheavens. Did she have to spell *everything* out for him? Skye held up her index finger. "One, we married in a hurry."

"Because of the will…" he corrected.

She continued, "Two, I fainted at Thanksgiving."

"Could have just been a long day. The stress of a big emotional announcement…"

She rolled her eyes at that. "Plus, as you recall, we ran into Faith yesterday coming out of the obstetrician's office. I am certain she saw what was in my hands."

"She didn't say anything to us, so why would she say anything to anyone else?"

He's right, Skye thought. From what she had noticed, Faith was a very private person herself. She was also his family. And the one thing Skye was learning fast was that the Lockharts circled the wagons whenever they thought one of their own might need anything. Like love. Support. Congratulations?

"Maybe she wouldn't, normally," Skye rushed on, trying hard not to notice just how damn kissable her new husband looked. "But would she if your parents mention to her they ran into us at dinner, and we were so busy making googly eyes at each other and kissing that we had no idea they were even in the restaurant with us?"

"'Googly eyes'?"

Darn Ron for putting that silly expression in her head! "Figure of speech. And you know where I am going with this. Travis, we can't be disrespectful of their feelings in this. It's enough we didn't tell them about getting hitched and the terms of the will. If we neglect to share this with them, too, and leave them to figure it out on their own, they're not going to be able to help but resent me and think I'm bad news for you."

"Is that what happened with Dex back in Chicago? His parents thought you led their son astray?"

It was exactly what had happened. Margaret and Franklin Stone had been so relieved when she'd lost the baby and the wedding had been called off.

She didn't know if the Lockharts would react the same way. Everything she'd heard about the famously loving and generous family said not—but you never knew. Particularly if they thought, even erroneously, one of their own had been hurt and/or taken advantage of.

Which meant, whether Travis realized it yet or not, the two of them had to be proactive here.

She drew a breath and then tried again, lowering her voice to a whisper, "Listen to me, Travis. Family is important. And now that we're going to be a part of each other's lives because we share a child, it's really crucial that I get off to a better start with your entire family. Especially your folks."

Finally, he seemed to be on the same wavelength with her. "So you think we should go ahead and tell them now?" he ascertained.

"Yes. But," Skye replied, offering a final caveat, "I don't want another big surprise announcement at a family gathering, with everyone all at once."

"You're right. That was way too much stress." He whipped out his phone and began to type something on it.

Skye moved closer but could not see the screen. "What are you doing?" she demanded, trying and failing not to be overbearing. "Who are you texting?"

"Hang on. *Done.*" He turned the phone so she could see the text being sent to everyone with a cell phone in the Lockhart Family message group. It said, Great news! Skye and I are expecting a baby on May 13th!

Chapter Thirteen

"You *texted* them the news?" Skye stared at her husband in shock.

Travis slid his phone back in his pocket. "Yeah. All at once. Now everybody knows, and we don't have to worry about anyone's nose getting out of joint because they were told first...or last."

"Oh my..." Skye murmured, sinking down on a nearby box.

"You're not going to faint again, are you?" He hunkered down in front of her, clasping her hands in his.

"No."

"Good." His broad shoulders relaxed in relief. "'Cause that's the last thing I want..."

His phone went off. It was a return text from his mom: INCREDIBLE NEWS!

Other messages quickly followed, all unerringly positive. More cousins! Emma said.

"I hadn't thought about that," Skye mused. She hadn't let herself go that far down the road of happily-ever-after. But now that it had been brought up… "Our baby is going to have a lot of family, not just me and you," she noted wondrously.

He nodded. "And that family is yours now, too."

As if on cue, another message came in. His mom messaged: Make Your Own Pizza Night at the ranch tomorrow. Can we count on you two to attend?

Travis turned to Skye, a question in his eyes.

She knew she had nixed the cookie-baking at the ranch the weekend before. But her baby was going to be part of this family, and so was she—no matter what eventually happened with her and Travis. Which meant she had to start getting to know them all a whole lot better now.

"Do you have to work tomorrow?" he asked, obviously recalling she'd been off the previous Friday.

"No. My supervisor insisted I take tomorrow off… in honor of us being newlyweds and all."

He grinned. "Nice of her."

"Yeah, it was."

"So…about the gathering at the Circle L…"

"Sure. I'd love to go," she told him, finally ready to take a leap of faith and really try to become part of the Lockhart clan. "As long as it is okay with you."

"Are you kidding?" He looked like he had just won the lottery. Laughing, he gathered her into his arms and held her tight. "Sounds great to me."

Skye went back to work and arrived home around eight that night. As exhausted as she had been the previous three days when she had worked a twelve-hour shift, she stayed up only long enough to have a glass of milk and catch up with Travis and Luna, then went on to bed.

They snuggled during the night.

She slept in late the next morning, at Travis's insistence, while he got up with Luna and then went on to work. So she didn't see him until he got home from work around four thirty that afternoon. He came in, looking surprisingly tense. "Have you looked at your email this afternoon?"

She'd been alternately baking a dessert to take to the party and doing some holiday shopping online, to little avail. She still had no idea at all what to get Travis for Christmas.

"No."

"Check it."

"Okay." She went to her laptop on the kitchen table, opened up her email and saw a new message from Realtor Cristal Ricci. It was a formal offer from Izzie Wheaton. "It says here she wants to pay 1.8 million for the entire property, in cash, with all inspection waived. With an immediate possession." Throat dry, she gazed up at Travis, who was standing against the counter, legs crossed, arms folded. "That's $200,000 less than what the subdivision developer has already offered us."

"Right."

"So we have to refuse it, according to terms of the will."

"Question is, do you want to let Izzie Wheaton know she's been outbid and hence, maybe spark a bidding war that could end up being pretty lucrative? Or just stick with our earlier decision not to sell until at least April?"

Her heart began to race. Obviously, he had been thinking about this. "What do *you* want to do?" This was the real litmus test.

He tossed the ball right back in her court. "You're the one who is pregnant and would be facing a move in the third trimester or after our baby is born if we wait. Selling now would mean moving out now—but then you'd be settled wherever you felt comfortable before the birth."

He was leaving too much solely up to her. She liked it better when they made their decisions together. "Honestly? I don't want to move right now."

"Good. 'Cause neither do I."

She continued thinking out loud, "But you're right— if we sold in April, it would be a very bad time for us to move out and leave Winding Creek, with me due to deliver the baby in mid-May."

He nodded soberly. "Agreed. But what options does that leave us…that are okay with you?"

Selling the ranch piecemeal was not one of them; she felt disloyal to the Braelochs even thinking about it. Even if, as Griff Montgomery had confirmed, that once they did meet all the requirements and officially inherit Winding Creek together, the property would be theirs, free and clear, and they would be able to do whatever they wished with the ranch.

"Well…" Skye said before she could stop herself. "Once we complete our four-month marriage and inherit, there is really no rush. We actually don't have to move out right away. After all, there is no mortgage on the ranch, no debts left that have to be paid, and we will still have whatever is in the interim maintenance fund the law firm is administering. Which should pay the taxes on the land and carry us at least until summer's end."

He came over to sit next to her. "You've been considering all the options, too."

Skye nodded. "I have." She knew that this was a big decision for them both, but she liked the arrangement they had now and did not want to see it changed. Which would make it very easy to reject the offer Cristal Ricci had proposed on behalf of Izzie Wheaton.

"Not too late to change your mind…" Travis teased as they turned into the long drive that led to the Circle L an hour later.

Beside him, Skye looked as happy as he felt. In the back seat of the quad cab, Luna appeared the same. Life these days just seemed to be getting better and better. And in a roundabout way, they had Walter and Willa's last will and testament to thank.

"The casual family dinners can get pretty rowdy." He winked.

Like him, she was wearing a sweater and jeans. Boots. She waggled her brows at him. "As opposed to Thanksgiving?"

The last time—the only other time—she had been

there with him. His body hardened as she continued to gaze at him admiringly. "That was pretty formal. With everyone dressed up and on their absolutely best behavior, including the kids." He drove along the familiar tree-lined lane. "*This* is at the end of a long week. The kids are going to be in the kitchen, too, helping construct their own individual pizza pies." He did his best to prepare her for the mess. "Which means the flour's going to be *everywhere*. Ditto for the sauce and other toppings."

Her eyes sparkled. "I think I can handle it, cowboy."

"Good." He slanted her another contented smile. "'Cause when the little ones get excited, the volume of the party gets turned way up."

She seemed to be anticipating the evening with his family as much as he. "But in a good way?"

"Yeah." He reached over to briefly squeeze her knee. "Unless someone accidentally knocks their pie onto the floor or something. Then tears can erupt. But they are usually short-lived."

Skye tucked in a loose end of plastic wrap around the magic cookie bars she had made for the adults' dessert. The graham cracker crust held a sweet vanilla filling covered with chocolate chips, pecans and coconut. The second platter held an array of Christmas tree-shaped sugar cookies topped with frosting stars and sprinkled with multicolored pieces of candy.

Her gaze sifting over his face, she asked curiously, "By the way, where do you cook all those pizzas?"

"We all got together last year and gifted Dad with

a brick pizza oven for the backyard. So we bake them out there."

Travis paused at the end of the lengthy line of parked cars. They were still a long way from the Circle L ranch house, but the width of the blacktop lane only allowed for parking along one side. "Do you want me to drive up and let you off?"

"Don't be ridiculous. I'm pregnant, not disabled. Besides, I would rather walk in together."

"Me too." He got Luna out of the truck and snapped on her leash, then walked around to relieve Skye of the desserts she'd been holding so she could get down from the cab.

She looked up at him, her slender shoulders squared as if for battle. "Which do you want me to take—Luna or the platters?"

Realizing how overwhelming his family could be— especially en masse—for anyone, never mind someone who had grown up an only child who was later orphaned and had gone on to live alone, he said, "Luna." Their pet had a calming effect on both of them.

She drew a deep breath and worked the leash from his palm, her silky fingers briefly brushing up against his skin in the process. Feeling her tremble, he asked, "Nervous?"

Skye swallowed. "A little. It's the first time I've seen everyone in person since we told them our big news via text. Plus, the last time I was here, I fainted!"

He chuckled and leaned over to kiss her brow. "An event that will go down in the Lockhart family story hall of fame, I am sure."

She tilted her head up, her usual good humor returning, just as he had hoped. "Okay. In retrospect, it is a little funny," she admitted, steering Luna to walk on her left side instead of in front of them.

As if realizing permission needed to be granted before they went inside, Luna sat. They paused just outside the front door, too.

Giving in to impulse, Travis cupped Skye's face with his free hand, then leaned down to kiss her. "Relax," he whispered against her lips. "The fam' already loves you."

Skye returned his kiss. When she drew back, she let out a shuddering breath. "You're sure?" she managed.

"Positive, darlin'." He smiled down at her tenderly. "Ready?"

"Yes," she finally said.

And when they walked in through the front door, they found out just how wanted she was.

The joyous shouts of "Welcome to the family!" sounding in her ears, Skye stared at the party banner strung across the living room of the Circle L ranch house that said Congratulations, Travis and Skye!

All the members of his family were there, and a pile of gifts were stacked on a table bearing their name.

She turned to Travis. He was as stunned as she was—and beaming. His grin spread even wider. "Give a couple a little warning, huh?" he complained good-naturedly. Everyone laughed and clapped, and the two of them were engulfed in hugs.

"Likely chance, after you already rejected the idea of a family wedding and/or reception!" Mackenzie said.

"And a baby shower, too!" Emma declared.

His family had wanted to do all that for them? Skye felt all the more stunned. She could understand him rejecting the ideas—at least those related to the wedding. But why hadn't he said anything to her?

Let her help decide?

Beside her, oblivious to her feelings, Travis was shaking his head and chuckling. "You say that as if I could have prevented an eventual celebration," he teased. He wrapped his mom and then his dad in warm, familial hugs. "'Cause we all know how these two get when they are determined to honor someone!"

More laughter followed, along with more warm embraces and a lot of excited chatter. Noah's eight-year-old daughter, the eldest of all the grandchildren, approached with shy resolve. "Come and see the Special Occasion yard sign Aunt Mackenzie made for you!" she said.

It was a pair of silver wedding bells inscribed with their names and the date of their nuptials.

More gifts followed: Sweet handmade cards from all the kids. Presents from all seven siblings and their spouses, and his parents. An embossed leather photo album for memories, including the snapshot Noah had taken of them on their wedding day. His three-year-old twins marched in with a bouquet that was an exact replica of the one Travis had brought her. Then, to top it all off, his parents gave them an ornament for their tree, with a photo of the two of them and the year beneath.

And suddenly, it was all too much. Skye burst into

tears and, horrified by her uncontrolled show of emotion, rushed from the room.

Behind her, she heard one of the grandkids explain, "Don't worry. Moms *always* cry when they're happy."

"She *is* happy, isn't she?" asked another.

Skye took refuge in the kitchen, then the long back hallway off that. Still crying, she darted outside and into the cold dark night.

Seconds later, Carol Lockhart was beside her. She had a cashmere throw for Skye to wrap around her shoulders. "Too much?" she asked softly.

Skye sniffed, still trying to pull herself together—which wasn't easy, given how completely overwhelmed she felt. She waved away her tears. "Everything you-all did was wonderful."

"Honey, *you're* wonderful. You have no idea how good it is to see Travis looking so happy."

She gulped and wiped her eyes, figuring this had to be said. "But, given how and why our union all came about—and now there's a baby involved—I'm surprised you-all don't think I somehow trapped him into this."

Carol laced a maternal arm around her shoulders, drawing her in close. "My son is self-reliant to a fault. If he got close enough to you to agree to marry you, for whatever reason, and have a baby with you, even if it wasn't exactly part of the plan, then it's because it was what he wanted. Because otherwise, believe me, none of this would have happened," Carol concluded. "None of it."

* * *

"Did you have fun tonight?" Travis asked hours later as he and Skye carried in the last of their cache of gifts and placed them all beneath their Christmas tree.

"I did." Skye hung up the homemade stockings bearing all three of their names on the fireplace mantel. *Once I got over that ridiculously embarrassing crying jag, anyway.*

"What about you?" She turned to study him. "Did my overwrought behavior embarrass you?"

"Nah." He lounged against the mantel, smelling like woodsmoke from the brick oven, soap and cologne. He also needed a shave, although she secretly liked the shadow of evening beard rimming his jaw. It made him look ruggedly sexy. "Everyone knows you're pregnant, and pregnant women are supposed to be really hormonal and, therefore, excessively sentimental. And that was what did you in, isn't it?" he said, straightening and coming closer. "All the stuff related to memories of our wedding day?"

Trying not to think about how intimate and right this all somehow felt, Skye nodded. "Yeah. That and the ornament that was so similar to the ones Walter and Willa put on their tree every year."

"My family didn't know about that," he admitted quietly. "They just wanted to help us commemorate the change in our lives and help us start our own traditions."

Which they had done.

He picked up an electric popcorn maker that Gabe

and Susannah and their kids had gifted them. "Interested in trying this out?"

Interested in trying a lot of things out. Not that she should be thinking this way. His offer had been purely platonic. Still, it was hard to be around him too long without wanting to ravish him. She smiled. "Sure."

He carried the new tabletop appliance into the kitchen. Skye followed with the jars of kernels, seasonings and oil that had been part of the gift. Luna trailed after them, still keeping a careful eye on Skye, though she had stopped crying long ago.

Travis opened the box, removed the parts and got out the instructions. "What do you want to drink with this?" she asked.

"Mmm. Whatever you're having."

"I'm having milk."

His sensual lips took on a pensive curve. "Milk sounds good."

His husky reply sending a thrill down her spine, Skye propped one hand on her hip and replied, "You know, you don't have to follow the same limits I am."

He winked, then measured out oil in the bottom of the pan and added half a cup of kernels. "You never know," he continued matter-of-factly, "I could be having pregnancy cravings."

Skye rolled her eyes and drew in another whiff of his tantalizing soap and cologne. As long as they were being good, maybe they could be a little bad, too. "Should I melt some butter to top that?"

He put the lid on, plugged it in and pressed the On button. The metal paddle in the bottom of the machine began to whir, moving the kernels over the heat source. He looked into her eyes, then flashed a grin. "Oh yeah."

Skye smiled. She, too, felt like she was getting everything she wanted and more this Christmas.

Watching all that was going on with the intensity of someone spectating at a tennis match, Luna sat back on her haunches, her expression comically perplexed. Then she jumped around in excitement as the kernels began to pop.

When the machine had finished, they took a big bowl into the living room, along with two tall glasses of milk and a chew bone for Luna.

They settled side by side on the sofa. The fire in the hearth and the beautifully decorated mantel and tree added to the festive air. Travis devoured his popcorn like a guy, a fistful at a time. Skye ate hers one kernel at a time. "This is delicious," he said.

She nodded. "Better than the stuff you get in a movie theater, that's for sure."

He shifted to face her, his expression curious. "So, what did you and my mother talk about when the two of you were outside?"

Chapter Fourteen

Skye turned to Travis and gave him the smile that always made his heart open wide. Her eyes were bright and full of light. "Carol said the family loves seeing you so happy."

"And she credits you with that?"

Skye nodded. "And the baby we have on the way."

Travis draped his arm along the back of the sofa and tucked her into the curve of his body. This was definitely the beginning of something magnificent. "Mom'd be right." He pressed a kiss on the top of her head. "I've never been this optimistic about the future."

"Me, either, strangely enough," she replied.

"Why do you say 'strangely'?" he asked curiously.

"Well, we have so much stuff about the future undecided. Like what we're going to ultimately do with the ranch, and when. And at what point should we honor our promise to each other and split up, at least in a legal sense?"

It felt good to be able to lean on each other, whenever, however, they needed. "Who says we have to split up?"

Their gazes met and she drew a breath. "I know how predestined this all feels right now."

Like larger forces are at play.

She frowned. "But ours is not a traditional marriage."

Tenderness sweeping through him, he leaned over to whisper in her ear, "Maybe that's a good thing, given how well things are going between us."

She shifted in the curve of his body, the softness of her breasts brushing against his chest. "You really think our arranged nuptials could work out over the long haul?"

His body hardening at the feel of her so close, he allowed matter-of-factly, "I think we've got as much chance as any newlywed couple to get everything figured out to both our satisfactions over the next year or so."

Her gaze narrowed. "You're counting on being married *that long*?"

And she wasn't?

Or was she just hedging her bets? Trying to protect herself from being hurt, the way she had been in her last relationship? Travis didn't know the answer. He decided it didn't matter. Her fears were not going to dictate their future. Reasonably, he pointed out, "We're not going to want to go through a divorce when we have a newborn to care for. We're both going to need to focus on our little one. And to do that right, we'll have to be a real team."

She paused a moment to let his point sink in. After a soft sigh, she admitted, "I never really liked having only one adult to count on after my parents died. I was always worried something would happen to my great-aunt Eileen…and then it did."

His heart broke at the thought of her alone. He knew firsthand how lousy it was to end up in the system, alone and scared, with no idea what your future held. He told her fiercely, "You don't have to worry our baby will end up in foster care, Skye. That will *never* be the case here. Our baby will have the two of us, plus my entire extended family."

She nodded and went back to eating popcorn. "Speaking of which," she changed the subject smoothly, "that was *quite the party* they threw for us tonight."

It had been. But there had been issues with that, too, that he was not sure he understood. "Enough to make you burst into tears."

"Happy, sentimental, completely overwrought ones," she said, obviously trying to make light of her earlier behavior.

He knew she wanted him to leave it alone. But he couldn't. "Why 'overwrought'?"

For a moment, he thought she wasn't going to answer—not candidly, anyway. Finally, she shrugged. "I know that was all business as usual for all of you, but I've never been part of such a big loving family, never mind celebrated any holidays or big events with them. Hence, it was a little overwhelming but in a good way."

"I see." Travis was relieved that was all it had been and that she wasn't upset about the other parties his clan had wanted to give, which he had rejected without even running by her first. Because for a moment there, when all the hoopla had been going on, he thought he had inadvertently made another big mistake. Glad he hadn't, he squinted at her. "By the way, what's our policy for gift-giving this first Christmas together?"

First Christmas. Had he actually said that aloud?

Judging by the expression on her face, he had.

She took a deep breath. "I wasn't sure if you were going to be on board with something like that or not," she said vaguely.

He tried not to feel too disappointed about that. Did she really see him as that unchivalrous?

"I didn't know if you would think that the baby was gift enough for both of us."

"Our baby is a wonderful gift," he told her. "But it doesn't need to be the *only* one we give each other."

She took a moment to consider that. "I see your point," she returned finally. "Your family and my co-workers and everyone we know is going to expect us to give each other *something.*"

The social expectation of others wasn't the reason he wanted to exchange presents with his wife. On the other hand, if that reasoning allowed him to gift her with what he had been thinking about since Walter and Willa passed, then so be it. "What did you have in mind?" he asked.

Excitement lit up her dark chocolate eyes. "Well, I thought we should possibly go in together and get Luna something."

"Agreed." He helped himself to more popcorn. "What about the baby?"

Abruptly, her expression became tense, and she worried the single piece of popcorn clasped between her fingers. "Would you mind if we held off on that right now?"

"Afraid it will jinx things?"

She bit her lip, then turned her gaze to his before letting out a quavering breath. "I really hate counting my chickens before they hatch, if you know what I mean."

"I do." It was why he had tried so hard, up to now, not to get too attached to anyone or anything.

"But we'll be making up for that in a few months," she continued with her customary enthusiasm, "when we start getting the nursery ready and all that."

He knew the further the pregnancy progressed, the better she would feel. "True. So what about the two of us?" He tucked an errant strand of hair behind her ear. "How do you want to handle that?"

"One gift—"

Only one? That was a lot of pressure to get it right, just out of the gate.

"—with a limit of fifty dollars or so?"

Even more pressure. Plus, he knew he had already spent more than that on supplies. But it wasn't like he could unbuild something that was already half-built.

So they'd just have to deal with that issue when or if it came up. He hoped it wouldn't. "Okay."

"Next question." She wrinkled her nose at him. "What would you like Santa to bring you this year?"

He chuckled. "Oh no." He waved a playful finger in her face. "I'm not going to do your thinking for you, darlin'."

She let out a dramatic groan. "Not even a single hint?"

"Not a clue. Except," he teased her gently, about to do what he had wanted to do for hours now, "maybe this…"

He bent down and captured her lips with his.

When she returned his kiss, it was everything he wanted. Sweetly tempting. Loving. Searching.

A rush of molten desire swept through him.

This was what he had always needed. *She* was what he had always needed, he thought as her soft, pliant body surrendered against him. And if Christmas wishes came true, she'd soon realize they belonged together, too.

Skye had come into this marriage thinking she would be able to leave it the same way—with her heart intact. Now she wasn't so sure. Every time Travis kissed her, yearning spiraled through her. The feel of his mouth on hers imbued her with the kind of loving devotion she had sought all her life. The kind only he could give.

And though she still wanted to protect herself, all she could think about whenever she was with him like this was how short life was. How unpredictable. The only thing she could count on, besides this very moment they were in, was how good she felt whenever she was with him. How cherished and respected and cared for.

And honestly, how could she turn away when he tasted so good? Felt so strong and so perfect for her in every respect? Skye groaned as he shifted her onto his lap, turning her so she was facing him, straddling his hips. A shiver of delight coursed through her as his hands slid beneath her sweater, unclasped her bra and cupped her breasts, his thumbs rubbing across the tender crests. She had never wanted someone so completely. Or felt so wanted in return.

Travis lifted his head. "Upstairs or downstairs?"

A walk on the wild side sounded just right. "I think right here sounds just fine," she purred.

Travis laughed wickedly, the way Skye had hoped he would. His gaze still holding hers, he stood her on her feet and divested her of her jeans and panties. Her sweater and bra went next. His clothes followed in fast order. Then they were back on the couch, and she settled snugly on his lap. Their mouths mated. She shifted her hips, encountering rock-solid hardness, heat and the power of his desire. His hands moved to the bare skin of her thighs, stroking, seducing.

"You feel so good," he rasped.

"So do you." She quivered as his caressing palms went even lower, finding the feminine heart of her with butterfly caresses. They kissed slowly and deliberately, both determined to find release. She shuddered again, so close to heaven, and he coaxed her to respond even more, to let all her inhibitions float away until she tightened her legs around him and melted against him.

She had time to draw one breath, and then his mouth was on hers again, hot and hard, and they were kissing as if their time together was never going to end. Her nipples budded. The skin between her thighs grew slick. He gripped her bottom and stroked her where their bodies met, and still they took their time, building their pleasure, propelling each other to the very depths of desire until there was no more waiting. He eased inside her, slow and sweet, claiming her as she claimed him. Giving and taking everything she had to give until they tumbled into the wonderful, shuddering abyss.

"The mailwoman was here already?" Skye asked the next morning as Travis came in, Luna by his side. It was barely ten o'clock! Usually, she didn't make her Saturday delivery till much later in the day.

"Yeah, I was surprised, too." He inclined his head at the Overnight Mail envelope in his hand. "She had a package that needed to be signed for. Luckily, Luna and I were already outside, so she didn't need to get out of her truck."

Skye put down her coffee cup. "What is it?"

"Beats me. All I can tell you for sure is that it's addressed to both of us, and there's a return Houston address for Izzie Wheaton." Travis handed it to her.

He stood beside her and watched while she opened it, then pulled out a single Christmas postcard, the kind families sent out with pictures of their kids. This one was divided into four sections, with the same group of people—Izzie Wheaton, her three kids, and oilman slash husband, Kirk. In one section, they were standing in front of their River Oaks mansion; another, in front of a gorgeous log cabin-style home in Aspen; and a third in front of a sprawling oceanfront beach house in Kiawah, South Carolina. The fourth quadrant was empty. Izzie had written in the space, "Imagine how great it would look if we had our Texas ranch, the Winding Creek, right here!"

On the back, the heiress had written, *Name your price!*

They both exchanged beleaguered sighs. "Not much of a negotiator, is she?" Skye said.

Travis frowned. "I think that's what Realtors and lawyers are for. But you are right." He paused to meet her eyes. "This is a little...weird. Not to mention pushy—"

"I know, right?" Skye agreed. "On the other hand, Cristal was very clear when she told us that no one says no to her very wealthy client. She always gets what she wants in the end."

"Well, Izzie Wheaton's going to be disappointed here," Travis said firmly as Skye put the mock-up of a holiday postcard aside.

His phone rang. "My brother." He put the phone to his ear. "Hey, Noah, what's up? Um... Let me ask." He put the call on hold, then said, "Noah needs help putting together a Christmas lawn display, and all three of his girls are in total meltdown. He wants to know if you and I can help. He said to bring Luna, too. She can keep their dog, Tank, company."

"Of course we'll help out." That's what families were for. "Do we need to bring anything?"

"Just my tools, and I can get those."

Fifteen minutes later, they were pulling up in front of Noah's ranch, a stunning glass-and-cedar abode built in a modern California style.

The nearby barn and detached garage were brand-new, too. Upon closer inspection, she saw the front lawn was littered with cardboard boxes and what looked to be part of Santa's sleigh.

When they got out of the car, Noah strode over, trailed by three very fussy little girls. The oldest, Lucy, had her arms folded across her chest, her every forward step a temperamental stomp. Behind her were the adorable twins. Avery seemed to be in charge of whatever their current mission was, and the sweet and mellow Angelica followed at her side while Tank, the family's chocolate Lab, remained on the front steps.

Travis looked at the number of boxes spread out over the grass, all marked as Christmas lawn ornaments. "Over your head?"

"You have no idea," Noah muttered, looking to them both for help. "Thankfully, I managed to get Dad and Cade and Zach to come over to lend a hand, too. I couldn't get any other female help on short notice, though."

Skye lifted a hand. "Not a problem. I can handle the three girls."

Lucy peered at her resentfully. "Does that mean

you'll help us decorate our ornaments for the tree even though Daddy already said we couldn't do it today, even after he promised that we could!"

"I said you couldn't do it while I was working outside," Noah corrected gently.

"Because the twins make too much mess and break stuff," Lucy said, and pouted.

"We do not!" Angelica and Avery said in unison.

"Girls…" Noah warned, looking like he was at his wit's end.

Luckily for all of them, reinforcements had arrived. Skye watched as three pickup trucks drove up the lane, Lockhart men at the wheel.

Figuring the sooner the men got to work, the sooner they would finish, Skye held out her hands and smiled at her young charges. "How about we all go inside? You can show me where everything is, and we'll come up with a plan that works for us all."

"You still coming over to my shop tomorrow afternoon to work on Skye's gift?" Zach asked Travis as the assembling of Santa's sleigh got underway.

His dad sent him an inquiring look.

"It's a surprise." Travis went on to explain. "Something that Willa and I dreamed up for Skye before Willa passed. At first, I was just going to give it to her and let her know it was something she could take with her after we both left the ranch, but then I realized it would also be a pretty good Christmas gift."

"It's not finished yet," Zach said. "But the craftsmanship is excellent."

"She'd probably love it even if it was a homemade wreck," Cade teased, grinning. "She's so sweet on him."

Travis wished that were the case. While he knew they had a hot sexual relationship, a fast-building friendship and a baby on the way they were both already crazy about, he wasn't sure they would ever make it in the long run—although that was what he wanted, he was beginning to realize. More than ever.

"Love can sneak up on you," Travis's dad agreed. "Especially when you least expect it."

Was that what he and Skye were feeling? Love? Their bond was definitely sexual. And they were becoming very good friends. But was that enough to bind them together past their arrangement and the birth of their child?

Travis couldn't say. He knew what would make it easier, though: money. The kind he didn't have—but would, if they sold the ranch.

"Skye says she wants to sell Winding Creek after the baby is born."

"What do *you* want?" Cade asked.

That was easy. "To stay."

"Have you talked to her about that?" Robert chimed in.

Travis turned to his dad. "Yes. Several times."

"And...?" Zach asked.

"She'd like to stay, but she's concerned about the ongoing expense and how it will impact our overall financial security."

"Have you thought about making it a working ranch

again?" his dad asked, steering Travis in the direction he had always wanted him to go.

"Yes, but that will cost money in the beginning," Travis admitted. Maybe more than they could scrape together.

"And Skye's not amenable to taking that kind of risk?" Zach gathered.

Travis unwrapped the pieces one by one and discarded the excess Bubble Wrap in an empty box. "Not in theory, no."

"Have you worked on a business plan?" Noah asked. "Sat her down and showed her the figures?"

Travis tightened a screw and admitted reluctantly, "Not yet."

"Why not?" Zach asked.

Travis shrugged. "For one thing, it's nowhere near finished right now. Second, her obstetrician said she needs to avoid stress."

Robert fastened two pieces together. "You think making the spread a working ranch will stress her out?"

Travis thought about Skye's reaction to risk thus far. "Yes. I mean, she was okay with us marrying because we both wanted to honor Walter and Willa's last wish, and it was a short-term thing. But anything long-term, she shies away from." And that was, he knew, increasingly a problem.

"Oh, girls, those ornaments are just gorgeous, don't you think?" Skye stood back a distance from the Christmas tree in their family room. It was now decorated with Styrofoam balls, covered in glitter and paint.

The three girls were a mess of the same but were very pleased with their yuletide artwork. "Your daddy is going to be so impressed by what you've created!"

The twins had already lost interest. "Can we go and play with our doll babies?" Angelica asked.

"As soon as we get you cleaned up, yes, you can." Skye helped them remove their aprons and wash their hands. Then the twins dashed off.

Lucy continued standing in front of the lit tree, staring at it critically. Wondering what was wrong, Skye approached her. Finally, the little girl turned to face her. "Which ones are the prettiest?" she demanded.

Taken aback by the ferocity of the question, Skye said, "I think they're all equally beautiful and special."

Lucy scowled. "You don't think mine are better?"

Now, that was a hard question to answer. There was a big difference between a three-year-old's artistic ability and an eight-year-old's. "I think yours have a sophistication that is really stunning," Skye said. And it was true. Lucy had painted stripes of color on some and on others used little stencils to apply the glue, then the glitter. Her sisters had just rolled all their ornaments in glue and glitter for an overall sparkly effect. Yet all had charm.

Lucy sighed in disappointment and followed Skye back to the craft area they had set up. "I wanted mine to be more special."

Skye began to clean up the mess on the kitchen table. "I think they are."

Lucy pouted. "I mean more special than being a twin!"

So *that* was the problem. "Is it hard being a big sister sometimes?" she asked gently.

Lucy teared up. "The twins get all the attention. They get whatever they want!"

Skye put a comforting arm around her shoulders. "And you don't?"

Lucy ducked her head. "Daddy says since I'm bigger, I have to understand."

"And you don't?"

Her eyes filling all the more, she shook her head. Skye cuddled the little girl in her arms. "I'm sorry that life is hard for you sometimes," she soothed. "But there are advantages to being the oldest daughter, you know."

Her attention caught, Lucy sniffed. "Like what?"

"You can do things the younger girls can't, like help me rustle up some lunch for the guys out there."

Lucy's face lit up. "You mean cook?"

Skye went to the fridge. "Let's see what we've got."

Plenty of stuff for sandwiches, as it turned out. Plus, ingredients for queso and ranch dip, and a nice veggie tray.

"Do you think you could help me out by standing on a chair at the sink and washing some carrots and celery and peppers?" she asked.

Lucy nodded enthusiastically. "I used to help my mommy cook before she got sick and went to heaven."

Travis had mentioned that Noah lost his wife two years before. "Your mother must have really liked you helping her."

Lucy sighed, recalling happily. "She did. Mommy said I was a really, really good helper."

"I think you are, too." Hoping to build on the more cheerful change in mood, Skye asked, "Well, then, since you're the expert, what kind of sandwiches do you think we should make?"

"All different kinds!" Lucy declared.

Skye let her lead the way. Half an hour later, they had a variety of sandwiches made and the dips set out. Lucy also wanted potato and tortilla chips, so they brought those out, too.

It looked like the men were getting close to being done, but Skye knew they had to be starving. She turned to Noah's daughter. "Since you're the oldest, do you want to go out and tell the guys their lunch is ready?"

"Yes!"

Skye helped her put on her coat, then watched through the window as Lucy went out and resolutely crossed the lawn. Both dogs, who had been lounging on the porch, jumped up to follow her. Unfortunately, by the time she got to the guys, the men had stopped working and were talking seriously. Their sober expressions had Lucy hanging back until Robert noticed her standing there. He opened his arms for a hug, and his granddaughter obliged. Tilting her head up, she delivered the message.

The men nodded.

Lucy dashed back to the house, running at top speed, and came inside. "They said they'll be here in a minute!" She whipped off her puffy coat. "They gotta finish their conversation first."

"About the sleigh?" Skye hoped they had all the parts necessary for completion, that none had been missing from the boxes.

"About money," Lucy said.

Money?

"Don't worry, Aunt Skye. Grown-ups always look kind of mad when they talk about 'finances'."

How does she know that? Skye wondered.

"My mommy and daddy used to have fights about money all the time." Lucy sighed. "But they always made up whenever Daddy said he was sorry. And he said Mommy could have what she wanted, after all."

Wow. Not exactly a good lesson to impart to a child. Was Noah's unhappy experience part of what had made Travis so initially reluctant to take the plunge into marriage?

Chapter Fifteen

Hours later, Skye and Travis were back at Winding Creek. They'd had dinner in town and picked up some thank-you cards to send to his family for all the gifts they'd generously given the other night. Now they were sitting in the living room, in front of a blazing fire, Luna curled at their feet. Christmas music played softly in the background. Their beautifully decorated tree exuded a nice piney scent. They'd had to improvise to do this here instead of the table, so they were using upside down baking sheets as lap desks.

He shifted his big body against the cushions next to her, exuding strength and warmth. "It's a good thing you made a list, because I can't remember who gave us what at the Welcome to the Family party."

Luna lifted her head, her tail thumping happily.

Grinning, Travis leaned over and scratched her behind the ears. She thumped all the more. Watching the tenderness flowing between the two of them, Skye could only imagine what a good daddy he was going to be. He was just so intuitive and gentle…

Forcing herself to get back on task rather than think about how deeply attracted she was to him, Skye finished writing the note for the electric popcorn maker, which they both clearly loved.

She handed it to Travis. He signed his name at the bottom next to hers, then went about addressing the mailing envelope.

As she reached for the next card, she slanted him a teasing glance. "It's second nature after years of being the bridesmaid, never the bride." These were the kinds of tasks she had always been assigned to help out with.

He nudged her knee with his, responding playfully, "You're the bride now…"

Yes, she was. And it felt unbelievably good. For however long it lasted.

"But you've also been awfully quiet since we got home. Which makes me wonder if something is on your mind that we need to talk about."

As it happens, there are a lot of things.

"Did something happen out at Noah's while we were outside?"

Skye grabbed another card. "Lucy is having a hard time."

"Because the twins get all the attention." He put the postage stamp on.

She paused in surprise. "You knew?"

Smiling ruefully, Travis leaned over and kissed her cheek. "Everybody knows. She complains about it constantly."

Skye shifted sideways on the sofa. "You don't feel for her?"

He made a face before casually going on, "Probably not in the same way you do, since I came from a large family and was usually the odd sibling out every time."

That hurt her just thinking about it. Her heart went out to him. Unable to help herself, she placed a palm over the curve of his broad shoulder. "No one paid attention to you?"

The corners of his lips turned up in the sexy way she loved. He leaned over and kissed the top of her hand before returning his attention to her face. "I think it was more that I never demanded attention."

"And the squeaky wheel gets the grease," Skye mused.

"Right. Eventually, I came to realize it was because, unlike Cade and Emma, who each went on to become famous in their own right—"

As a footwear designer and pro baseball player.

"—I was happiest living life outside of the limelight."

Her chest aching with emotion, she gazed into his eyes. "What about the rest of your siblings?"

"They were all focused on achieving their goals. So as long as they were successful in that, they were happy. They didn't need to be a star."

"I'm not sure that Lucy will go that route. She really wants to be the star—or at least, she thinks she does now."

"It's understandable." Travis's face gentled sympathetically. "She was Shelby's right-hand gal until she died."

"What happened?"

His expression turned brooding. "Shelby had breast cancer that was discovered around the time she gave birth to the twins," he recollected. "It had been successfully treated. She'd had a lumpectomy and radiation and was given a clean bill of health."

"That's good," Skye said.

Travis nodded. "That's the hell of it. It was all good. She was trying to get her strength back after treatment. She had taken up running for an hour every morning with a group of female friends while Noah stayed home with the kids. Next thing he knows, he's getting a call that Shelby tripped and hit her head on the curb. An ambulance was called right away, but there was nothing they could do—the damage was so massive. She was already gone by the time she reached the hospital."

Skye's hand flew to her throat. "Oh my God."

"Yeah." Travis shook his head. He continued in a low voice laced with grief, "It was pretty awful. To think you had dodged a death sentence, only to go down in such a senseless way."

"So Noah moved back here."

"Not right away. He gave it a year or so in California. But he eventually realized they all needed to be a lot closer to family as well as have a complete change of scenery. So my dad sold him a hundred acres of Circle L land, and he built a house on the property a lot like the home they had left in California. As well as a barn and a stable so the girls could have pets if they wanted."

"So they've been in Texas a year, and Shelby has been gone for two."

"A little over that, yeah. Anyway, we all think Lucy's unhappiness stems from her missing her mom and that the twins are just a ready target."

It made sense. "Do the three of them *ever* get along?"

"Yeah. They do. But lately, there's been this under-current of escalating tension that Noah's doing his best to allay. It's why he let the girls talk him into such an outlandishly large yard display. He thought it would be a welcome distraction."

"It *was* beautiful, though." With Santa in his sleigh packed full of presents, and eight reindeer.

Travis shook his head. "Much more than he would have preferred, though."

Skye thought about what else Lucy had said. "Be-cause of the cost?" The question was out before she could stop it.

Travis gave her an odd look, letting her know that whether she meant to or not, she had overstepped a boundary. "Why would you say that?" he asked.

Travis figured it was a fair question. But Skye looked embarrassed.

"I'm sorry." She started to rise.

He caught her wrist and pulled her back down beside him. He could tell by the guilty, upset look on her face there was more. He didn't like it when she held stuff back from him. "What else happened?"

"It's nothing."

He tracked the spill of honey-brown hair over her shoulders; the strands that were a lighter gold, close to her face. "I disagree. Did Lucy say something else to you that she probably shouldn't have?"

Her cheeks flushed. "When I sent her out to get you-all for lunch, I had no idea you were in the midst of a serious conversation."

This could not be good. "What did she overhear?"

Skye paused a moment, as if trying to figure out how to phrase what she was about to reveal. "She said you-all looked upset because you were talking about money. But that it was okay because grown-ups always got mad when they had fights about money."

None of this was making any sense. "Where would she get that idea?"

"Apparently, Noah and Shelby fought about finances. A lot."

Travis hadn't known that. But then, his brother had never talked much about what was wrong in his life, only what was right.

He felt for his young niece, though. To have so few memories of her late mom—and for that to be even one of them...

"It had to be hard." He could only hope that he and Skye would not have similar conflicts about money.

"The honeymoon over already?" Ashley teased as they all gathered in the conference room the following Friday for morning report. The week had been a long one for Skye since she had worked twelve-hour shifts on Sunday, Tuesday, Thursday and now Friday, too.

Skye set her Travis-made breakfast down in front of her, along with the thermos of ginger tea he had specially prepared for her. "Was I frowning?" she asked in surprise. "I didn't realize that."

"What's on your mind, young bride?" Ron teased, sitting opposite her.

"It's way too early in your newlywed life to be down in the doldrums, especially during the Christmas holidays," Hailey agreed.

Skye glanced at the clock on the wall. They had about fifteen minutes before the night staff came in to update them on their patients. She figured her coworkers were as good a sounding board as ever.

With a sigh, she took the top off her yogurt parfait. "Travis and I agreed we should get each other gifts this year, and I don't have a clue what to get him."

"What are the parameters?" Ron asked.

Skye sipped her tea. "We said fifty dollars."

"Do you think he's being cheap?" Hailey frowned. "Is that the problem?"

"No, Travis isn't cheap," Skye huffed in exasperation. "Far from it. In fact, he is the most generous man I've ever met."

"Now *that* sounds like a newlywed." Hailey grinned.

"Is this the first time you'll be formally exchanging gifts?" Ron said, getting them back on track.

"Yes. We… Well, it never came up before. So, anyway, I've been thinking all week and trying to subtly quiz him about this and that, but he doesn't seem interested in anything I've mentioned so far."

"Like what?" Ashley ate her omelet.

"Oh, a new leather band for his watch or something 'cowboy' from Monroe's Western Wear. Or new floor mats for his truck…"

This caused a hoot of hilarity from all three. "I think you might want to go a little more personal than that," Ashley said kindly.

"I've been trying." Skye spooned up another bite of yogurt, fruit and granola. "I just haven't been getting anywhere." She frowned again in frustration. "And it isn't just the dollar limit we set. It's the category."

"Maybe you need to try a different tack," Hailey said. "What was your aha moment with Travis?"

Skye blinked. "My what?"

"Your aha moment. You know, the moment where you looked at him and you just knew he was the one for you."

Had she had that? Certainly there had been times when her heart had practically stalled in her chest: The first time they kissed. The first time they made love. And other times, too. Like the night they rescued Luna from the road and took her home, and both knew she was family to them. And then, of course, there had been the moment when she realized she was carrying his baby. And when they first heard their little one's heartbeat…

"Well, she's looking all dreamy again," Ashley teased. "So that tells me we're on the right track here—even if she won't yet share with us what her aha moment was."

"Hey, sometimes a person just knows," Ron cut in

with his man's point of view. He thumped his chest above his RN tag in the region of his heart. "Sometimes it's not all fireworks and pizzazz but something slow and wonderful."

"Talking about your love for your wife now?" Hailey said with a grin.

"Darn straight I am," Ron said. He turned to Skye. "If you want my advice on what constitutes a good gift, just pay attention to what your spouse wants and needs. Give them something that shows thought and care. And is equal to your feelings for them."

Skye thought back to the previous night. She and Travis had made love and then slept, wrapped in each other's arms, in her bed. Trouble was, her full-size mattress wasn't really big enough for his large frame, even when they were snuggled close together. A couple of times, he had almost fallen out during the night. Yet he never complained about being uncomfortable or wanted to go back to his own bed, in the guest room down the hall. Which, even though it was queen-size, was also really too small…

She thought about how he always had dinner waiting for her when she got off work. How he got up with her before dawn every workday to see her off, even when he didn't have to. She knew it was past time she went all out for him, too.

"Hey," Skye told Travis that night when they met up after her shift was over to attend the holiday choral festival in the town square. "I've had second thoughts about the dollar limit on our presents for each other."

Travis paused. "Higher or lower?"

She handed him the peppermint cocoa she had purchased. Her pretty eyes glittered with excitement. "How about just…none?"

Wanting to make sure he understood her, he said, "You want us to have no limit, price-wise?" He tried not to do a little hallelujah dance.

She stood on tiptoe and kissed his cheek. "Well, you know what they say in Texas, cowboy. Go big or go home. And I'm starting to think we should celebrate the baby we have on the way and go big."

Okay, obviously she had something in mind. Something that was making her happy just thinking about it.

Just that swiftly, Travis knew what he wanted to get her. Even if it was a risk. "I can go big," he said.

"Good. And one more thing." She turned serious. "I might have to give you your present a little bit early, say on December 23. And you might have to stay away from Winding Creek all day while I'm getting it here."

He looked down at her. "You're not buying me a horse, *are you*?"

She looked panicked. "Did you *want* a horse?"

"No!" At least not yet. "It was a joke! I was just referencing all those questions you've been asking me lately about what kind of cowboy things I liked at Monroe's Western Wear…"

She still looked a little shell-shocked.

He kissed her temple, felt her relax and continued to set her straight. "But just to be clear, I do not want a horse. Although I can see us having a few when our baby is old enough to learn to ride."

"Me too." Skye smiled. "I think that would be great."

He laced his arm through hers, and they walked through the park, enjoying all the decorations, listening to the beautiful Christmas music permeating the night air. All those voices, from every choir in the area, raised in song.

Loving the contentment he felt whenever they were together like this, he leaned down to whisper in her ear, "So, back to the gift you have in mind for me. Are you going to give me any hints about what it might be?"

"Nope. Not a one. You need to be as surprised and happy as I want you to be."

"I want that for you, too." He pulled her off the path and turned to her, bringing her close enough to kiss.

"Then it's settled?" Skye asked when their sweet and tender lip-lock ended.

Travis nodded. "December 23 sounds fantastic for our first gift exchange."

And if everything went the way he wanted, it definitely would not be their last.

Chapter Sixteen

Travis insisted Skye sleep in on Saturday morning, so it was nine o'clock before she got up, showered and got dressed for the day.

As she walked out of her bedroom, the delicious smell of pancakes and bacon wafted up from downstairs.

But the thought of all she had to do that day had her moving away from the staircase. Past Travis's small guest quarters and the queen-size bed that had not been slept in as of late; the bathroom he used; and then the room that held all the boxes of memorabilia that Willa had been trying to sort at the time of her death, which she and Travis still hadn't had the heart to go through.

At the far end of the hall was the master suite. The room had been emptied of the twin hospital beds and other medical equipment at the same time the chair lift had been removed from the staircase. As per Walter and Willa's wishes, everything had been donated to other seniors in need. Now the large room stood empty, the peach walls a reminder of all that had been.

For months now, Skye had stayed away from this room. And the memories it evoked.

Now she knew it was time to move on… Turn the next page in their lives. She knew it was what Willa and Walter would have wanted, too.

"Everything okay?" Travis's voice rumbled behind her.

He had already showered but not shaved. The rim of beard on his jaw perfectly enhanced his chiseled features, and the happy twinkle in his amber eyes made her think about how much joy he had brought to her life. She went up on tiptoe and pressed a good-morning kiss to the line of his jaw.

"Yeah." She inhaled his brisk masculine soap and minty toothpaste, then put her heels back flat on the floor. "I was just thinking."

He tilted his head, still surveying her curiously. "About…?" he prodded in the soft, sexy voice she loved so much.

If she told him, it would give away her plans. So she blurted out the first fib that came to mind: "I was just trying to see the master suite through a potential buyer's eyes, think about what needs to be done."

Her words brought forth an immediate frown on Travis's face. "There's no rush, is there? Since we're not selling until after the baby is born and our lives are settled?"

But he needed more space now, Skye thought. Especially if his current room was going to be used as a nursery if they did stay on through the summer—and maybe fall, too.

Adapting her best poker face, she cast one last look at the room and turned back to him with a smile. "You know me. Always thinking ahead."

And planning to repay all your kindness and give you the best Christmas gift I possibly can.

Half an hour later, they had finished eating and done the dishes.

As Skye gathered up her shoulder bag, phone, keys and jacket, she sent him a regretful look. "I'm sorry I can't stick to the regular plan and do errands and share chores with you today."

Travis was bummed, too.

They had recently started spending their Saturdays together because it was the one day a week they both didn't have to work.

"But with Christmas just ten days away," she continued ruefully, "and my shopping still not done..."

He let his gaze drift over her. What they said about pregnant women having that special glow was true; she seemed to get more beautiful every day. Figuring they would make up for lost time later, he hugged her warmly. "Not to worry. I haven't had time to buy your gift, either," he teased.

She wrinkled her nose at him, her eyes taking on a playful gleam.

Resisting the powerful urge to take her by the hand

and go back upstairs to bed, he said, "Just so we don't run into each other, where are you planning to shop?"

Skye raked her teeth across her lower lip. "San Angelo, I think. Depends on if they have what I need or not." He helped her with her coat, lifting the veil of her hair out of her collar and doing it again when she put on her scarf. "What about you? Where will you be?"

Knowing that finding the perfect gift for her was going to be his pleasure, he said, "I'll most likely be in Laramie. Depends on if they have what I need or not, too."

She briefly pursed her lips before asking, "But you'll let me know if you head my way? I don't want to run into each other and spoil the surprise."

"Promise." He caught her and kissed her lingeringly. She melted against him, and he loved the way that felt, as well as the closeness that seemed to increase with every hour they spent together.

The moment in the master suite, when she'd seemed to be holding back what she was feeling and thinking ahead to the time they'd be splitting up, was probably nothing to worry about.

Skye was just preparing for every possibility, the way she always did.

It didn't mean their relationship was already starting to cool like his previous serious involvement had. He just had to keep taking it day by day, same as her, and let the baby and the magic of Christmas continue to bring them together.

Shortly thereafter, they went their separate ways. Travis headed for the town's best jeweler, who was also one of the premier artisans in west Texas. He talked with her about what he wanted to give Skye for their first Christmas together, as well as what he hoped it would mean to both of them. She sketched out several ideas. He chose the one that most suited his wife and arranged to pick it up on December 22.

From there, he went to Callahan Custom Carpentry, where he had been working on another surprise for her for several months now. It was a kitchen island, with storage cabinets on one side and a place to sit and eat on the other. With Zach's assistance and advice, he had built it out of a gorgeous walnut. The base had been painted to match the newly refinished sage green kitchen cabinets in the ranch house. The top was going to be a beautiful butcher block. And it was nearly done, as were the four ladder-backed stools. Once it was in, Skye would have the prep space she'd yearned for. And if she decided she didn't want to stay, well, then she could take it with her as a remembrance of their time together at Winding Creek.

Zach brought out the grape-seed oil. He handed Travis a soft cloth. "You're going to need to put three coats of this, twenty-four hours apart," he said.

"Got it. Thanks." Travis worked off the lid, then carefully began to spread the oil over the top of the island.

"So, how are things going with Faith and Quinn?" Quinn was their eighteen-month-old son.

"Good. Quinn has been talking about Santa and baby Jesus nonstop." Zach chuckled as he worked on his own project, an old-fashioned wardrobe. "How about you and Skye?" he asked. "And the dog you're fostering?"

And hoping to formally adopt, Travis added silently. Although in their minds, Luna was already theirs. "All good, too."

"It just might work out, you know." Zach winked. "Stranger things have happened."

Travis chuckled. "Like your marriage to my sister?"

Zach laughed. "Hey, it was *Faith* who looked at me as the enemy when we first met."

"That's because she didn't expect Quinn's biodaddy to show up just days before she was set to adopt."

"And I didn't expect to fall in love with the foster mother of my son. But we did. And it's been pure heaven ever since."

Finished rubbing in the oil, Travis stepped back to wait the required fifteen minutes before he could buff the surface. He turned the conversation back to his own love life. "Our situation is a little more complicated."

"Because of the baby on the way?"

"And the terms of the will." He filled Zach in on the dilemma regarding selling Winding Creek in the spring and how it would prove to be difficult timing with the birth of the baby. "Skye and I have been talking about staying at Winding Creek through summer's end. Just to make things easier."

"And then what, will you buy another place together?" his brother-in-law asked.

"Not clear." Travis sighed. "Although she's indicated she won't leave Laramie County or move far away from me and/or the rest of my family. She wants us all in the baby's life."

Zach lifted a brow. "But beyond that, she won't commit?"

"No."

"What do *you* want—if you could have whatever you wished?" his brother-in-law pressed.

"To stay on the ranch and bring it back to life and raise a family there. With her. And our baby and any others we might have."

Zach nodded, impressed. "Dream big."

"This *is* Texas," he deadpanned. "And you know what they say—if you can dream it, you can do it."

"Have you told her any of this?"

"I've tried. But she has a tendency to worry." *Especially when life begins to feel a little too perfect.* "So we're kind of taking it one day at a time."

Zach sympathized. "And you're not comfortable with that plan?"

It reminded him of his ex, how Alicia was when the house they were rehabbing was nearly finished. Before they found out how much they would recoup in selling it. Before they broke up. When he realized it was their business partnership holding them together—at least in her view—and not love. Although in retrospect, Travis wondered if he had ever really loved Alicia or if it had truly been convenience, a mutual goal and hot sexual sparks keeping them going for as long as they had.

He shrugged. "I guess I want more than Skye does out of our situation."

Zach went to the small fridge in the corner and got out two beers. He handed one to Travis, worked the cap off his own. "Then you're going to have to really get serious about showing her just how committed to having a future with her you are." He gave his brother-in-law a confident look. "But knowing you, I'm sure you're already formulating a plan that will allow you to achieve what you want."

He was. "I want to expand my handyman service. But bringing someone on will cost money, at least in the beginning. Plus, I'd have to find some guys or gals who are interested in doing that kind of work."

"Have you thought about going over to the West Texas Warriors Association in Laramie, talking to the military veterans there? That's where I found my employees. The WTWA has job-training grants you can apply for, too. They underwrite the cost of apprenticeship for a couple of months, which is usually enough to get someone educated on the basics of the job."

Travis took a draught of beer. "That's a good idea."

Zach paused to text him the information. "Anything else Faith or I can help you both with?" he asked.

Seeing enough time had elapsed, Travis grabbed another cloth and began to buff the island's butcher block top. He shook his head. "Not that I can think of, thanks." Like his wife, he was just trying to enjoy the holidays. Build on everything they were beginning to feel and go from there.

Skye had to go to three stores to find exactly what she wanted for the first part of Travis's gift. She grabbed a salad for lunch, then spent the rest of the afternoon going from store to store in search of the second part, to no avail. Nothing seemed exactly right for him. But she wasn't discouraged. There were still plenty of places to look online.

Thankfully, finding the third and last part of his gift was much easier.

She was halfway home when a call came through from Travis asking if she wanted to meet at the Wagon Wheel restaurant in town. Her stomach rumbling in agreement, she said she'd love to, and he told her he'd get a table and see her there.

Travis was waiting when she walked in. She noticed he had shaved and put on a fresh set of clothes. When he stood to help her with her chair, she teased, "Such a gentleman."

"Hey." He angled a thumb at his chest. "I was raised right."

She batted her lashes at him. "You sure were."

The waitress came by, and they placed their orders. He held her hands and gazed into her eyes as if he hadn't seen her in forever. "So, how was your day?" he asked huskily.

Damn, she had missed spending the entire day with him. She didn't realize until this moment just how much. "Good. And yours?"

His eyes crinkled at the corners. "Very productive."

This was getting exciting. *He* was exciting! She tilted her head at him. "Going to give me any hints, cowboy?"

"Not a one, darlin'." Travis winked.

"And the rest of your day…?" She couldn't imagine he'd spent the entire time shopping. He was a man, after all. Also, he was very efficient in everything he did.

Travis's expression changed. He exhaled roughly, admitting, "I could have done without the texts and phone messages from Izzie Wheaton."

Skye blinked and looked down at her phone. Nothing. "Izzie contacted you?" she asked, stunned.

Travis nodded, looking even grimmer. "She tried. Repeatedly. She didn't call you and leave messages, too?"

"No." She checked her phone again to make sure. "Not once."

He seemed really irritated, which meant it couldn't be good. "What did she say?"

Travis released his hold on her and sat back.

"What she's *been* saying," he muttered. *"'Name your price.'"*

"How did you respond?"

He sipped his water, his expression maddeningly inscrutable. "I didn't. I wanted to talk to you first."

The thought of leaving the ranch was suddenly a very unsettling one. She didn't want anything to interrupt the closeness she and Travis were building. And she really didn't want a woman like Izzie Wheaton playing her and her husband against each other.

Skye's throat grew tight. "We've already told her no. That we weren't doing anything official until spring or later."

"Right."

She took a sip of water, hoping to ease the tension. "Why should we be forced to repeat the same thing again and again?"

One corner of Travis's mouth lifted slightly. He inclined his head as if in complete agreement.

Having dealt with spoiled women before—and very irritated with the heiress for having interrupted her husband's day—Skye continued thinking out loud, "Plus, if we respond to Izzie's constant pleas, all we're really doing is just inviting further dialogue on a situation that isn't going to change."

"Agreed." Looking relieved, Travis took her hand in his. "Now," he said in that tough-tender tone she adored, "where were we…?"

And just like that, their dinner date happily resumed.

Chapter Seventeen

Skye worked at the hospital on Sunday, putting in an extra two hours at the end of her shift so a colleague could see her daughter's Christmas pageant.

She'd already eaten dinner at the hospital, but when she walked in the door, she saw that Travis had a fire blazing and soup heated up for her, just in case. Luna cuddled up next to her, too, as they consumed bowls of creamy, delicious potato soup studded with crispy bits of bacon and sharp cheddar, and talked about their days.

Too soon, she was nodding off.

Travis insisted she go to bed. She was asleep the moment her head hit the pillow but woke during the night to find his big body curled around hers—which, as it turned out, was the only way he could fit in the bed with her...

The next morning, she woke refreshed, in time to make him breakfast before he headed off to work a full slate of handyman projects for customers.

With only eight days left until Christmas, she went out to her car and brought in the stuff she had purchased at the San Angelo hardware store.

Luna followed her from room to room, her tail wagging, gazing up at her in anticipation. "I know, girl. It's time to get to work."

Travis worked straight through lunch in order to get home earlier. He had promised Skye he would pick up dinner at Sonny's Barbecue, and it was just after five when he turned into the ranch.

That time of year, it got dark a lot earlier. Even earlier on gloomy wintry days like the ones they were having. He was expecting to see the lights blazing on the first floor of the ranch house.

Instead, the windows were dark. The only ones that appeared to be lit were the ones in the unused master bedroom on the second floor.

Wondering what in the heck was going on, he left the take-out bags in the kitchen and headed up the stairs. Luna met him at the top, a quizzical expression on her face. As if she were trying to tell him something odd was going on. "Skye?" he said, beginning to panic. Had something happened to her or their baby?

The beagle turned to lead the way. He followed her rapidly down the hall. "Skye?"

She appeared in the doorway, wearing an old

sweatshirt, sneakers and jeans that were now dotted with paint.

"What are you doing?" he demanded before he could stop himself.

"Um…" She apparently had to stop and think about how to answer that. Then, with a wave, motioned for him to follow her. "Come in and see."

He strode in to join her in the center of the empty master suite. The peach paint was gone. In its place, a bluish-gray color that was in a lot of his plaid shirts.

She held up a hand. "Not to worry. As you can tell, the paint has no fumes—it was made to be safe for pregnant women, kids and pets." She flashed a mischievous grin. "And, of course, men, too."

"When did you decide to do this?" He walked around. She had done a beautiful job—even refreshing the white trim, too.

"Saturday."

She had kept it a secret all this time? Battling equal parts hurt and wonder, he asked, "Why didn't you tell me?"

She straightened to her full height. "I wanted it to be a surprise."

It was that, all right. Was this a message to let him know he really wasn't all that necessary in her life? That, baby or no, she intended to be as independent as ever?

Travis had no idea. What he did know was that he didn't want her tiring herself out unnecessarily. He moved closer, inhaling the uniquely feminine fragrance that was all her. "If you wanted the room painted, darlin', I would have done it for you."

To his surprise, Skye threw her head back and laughed—a delightful musical sound. "That's the thing, cowboy… I wanted to do it for *you*."

He blinked, not sure what she meant. He skimmed her upturned face, realizing all over again just how darn pretty she was. "Why would I care if the walls were newly painted or not?"

"Well." Again, that long pause. The one that said she was thinking up something to say instead of just answering honestly from the heart. Finally, she let out a shy sigh. "I was hoping you might want to move in here since it's a lot larger than the room you're currently in."

The room he was currently "in" was right next to hers. Not that he did much more in there than change clothes these days… "I'm fine."

She scoffed. "You barely have room to walk between the nightstand and the bed. There's not even a dresser in there."

"I've got everything I need in the small closet and on those shelves." Plus, he had been sleeping with her, even though her bed was really too small for the both of them. It sure made cuddling great, though. He studied her. "There's some other reason."

She blushed. Guilty as charged. "I was hoping we might eventually turn the smaller room that you are in now into the nursery. And if we're going to put the house on the market eventually, every room will need to be a neutral color."

"Like the ivory paint on all the walls downstairs."

"Right. That blue gray you like so much is considered neutral, too."

While he was happy she had put so much thought into it, it bummed him out that she had shut him out of the decision-making process. He'd felt—perhaps erroneously—like they were a team now. "You still should have let me do this."

"I like painting, remember? It was how I worked my way through college. And I did interior painting for Walter and Willa, too."

He remembered Willa talking about that.

She had known how Skye liked to stay constantly busy, and Willa had worried that their private duty nurse didn't have enough to do. She had let Skye take on small home-improvement projects to fill up the hours and give her additional cash. "Do you want me to paint the storeroom and the nursery, then?"

Skye shook her head. "I have no idea what color the nursery is going to be yet, and we're going to have to clear out all the boxes in the storeroom first."

He searched for something she would agree to let him do. "I can move them."

She nixed that idea with a lift of her delicate palm. "I don't want to do that until we go through them and figure out what we should keep and what should go to the local historical society. And I'm not up to that yet."

He wasn't, either, truth be told. The grief over losing Walter and Willa was still pretty intense. He didn't feel it all the time anymore. But when he did, it was still like an arrow to the heart. He knew it was the same for her. "I understand," he told Skye gently. "We can definitely wait until we are both ready to go through the rest of their personal stuff."

"Thank you."

"I still wish you would leave all the heavy lifting to me," he grumbled. "That's what husbands and daddies are for, you know."

To his frustration, she made no effort to promise she would. She tipped her head up to him. "What do you think of the color?"

"I like it. A lot. And in fact," he teased her, "I like you, too." He took her into his arms and guided her against him.

She wound her arms around his neck and gazed up at him adoringly. "You know, cowboy," she bantered right back, "it might surprise you, but I kind of figured that…"

He chuckled. "Are you sure?" He sifted one hand through her hair, drawing her ever nearer. "Because I am ready and willing and able to persuade…"

"I was hoping you'd say that," Skye murmured against his lips. He kissed her. She kissed him back. Again and again. Until they made their way down the hall, ending up in his bed this time.

Their lovemaking was as spectacular as always. When the fireworks faded and he held her close, he realized, with a tiny bit of frustration, that this was the only time she totally let down her guard and gave herself over to him completely.

The rest of the time, she seemed to be holding tight to some sort of secret exit plan.

That was typical Skye: Hope for the best and prepare for the worst.

Maybe he was a little like that, too.

And yet, to his growing satisfaction, each time they did come together like this, they got closer. Which meant there was only one path to the goal he desired. He would have to keep right on making love to her every opportunity he had. And enjoy the heck out of it when she loved him right back.

On Tuesday, Skye worked at the hospital, and Travis used the extra time at the end of his workday to put the final coat of grape-seed oil on the kitchen island he had built for her. Afterward, he went home and took Luna out for some exercise. They were just finishing up when Skye drove up to the house. She got out, a pizza box in hand. "Looks like dinner, girl," he told Luna.

They rushed over to help his wife with her belongings. He set the table in the kitchen while she went upstairs to change. She came down in her pajamas, face scrubbed, hair swept up. She had never looked more beautiful.

"Do you want milk or water?"

"Milk, please."

He poured two glasses, then joined her at the table, pleased to see that she had gotten their favorite pizza with all the toppings except for jalapeños, which were only on his side.

"Heartburn?" he asked.

"Hope not. Hence, the reasons for the proactive measures."

"Since you're off tomorrow, are you up for a little joint Christmas shopping?"

She looked pleased by the prospect of spending time together. "What are we going to shop for?"

"Lockhart-family gifts."

Her hand flew to her mouth. "Oh yes. I should have realized…"

He covered her hand with his, stopping her mid-apology. "So should I, if we're going down that road. But I've been so busy enjoying married life that I hadn't given it much thought. Lucky for us, Emma texted me a reminder."

Looking a little overwhelmed again by all the Lockhart-family stuff, Skye paused, a slice of pizza halfway to her lips. "Do we need to buy gifts for everyone?" she asked carefully. Apparently already jumping ahead to the planning phase.

"No. That would be ridiculous. Eight siblings, spouses, kids…"

"Yeah," she admitted after a sigh, "it would be a lot."

"What we've been doing is, each person coming to dinner on Christmas Day brings one gift, and it has to be under twenty dollars. Guys bring something for a guy. Gals bring something for a gal. Kids bring something for a kid. And we do the pets, too. Then we mix them up under the tree, and they get passed out to all the attendees after dinner."

She smiled. "Sounds fun."

"The siblings each also get gifts for Mom and Dad. This year, of course, the gifts will be from the two of us."

"So we're going to need five gifts." She continued with a thoughtful smile, "Do you have any ideas?"

He shared his thoughts, and she chimed in with

some suggestions of her own. It made him feel good to work together as a team on this.

She smothered a yawn, for the first time evidencing the long day she'd had. "When did you want to go shopping tomorrow?"

"I was thinking early afternoon. There are a couple of jobs I have to get done in the morning, but after that, I can take the rest of the day off. And this way, you can sleep in, catch up on some Z's."

She clasped his hand. "Don't want me getting up to make you breakfast and see you off?"

He loved when she did that. It was the best way ever to start the day. But he wanted to take care of her more. "I want you—and the baby—to get some extra sleep." He lifted her hand to his lips and kissed the inside of her wrist. "Think you can do that for me?"

Her eyes took on an immensely happy glow. "Going all protective on us?"

"You bet." He leaned over to kiss her, knowing that taking care of her and the baby was the most important responsibility he would ever have.

Skye woke at ten the next morning with the realization Christmas was nearly here, and she had never been happier in her life. She looked over and saw Luna sleeping on the dog bed they had set up for her in the corner of her bedroom. Travis was gone. She hadn't heard him leave. She remembered very well how it had felt to make slow and tender love with him and then sleep wrapped in his arms.

Eager to get her day started—and to find out if the

second present she had ordered for Travis was going
to be delivered that day, as expected—she got out of
bed and went to find her computer tablet.

Unfortunately, instead of the delivery-tracking
email she had wanted to find, there was a cancellation
notice instead.

Item out of stock. Your credit card will not be charged.

"Oh no!" Skye looked at Luna. "We can't give him
the first present without the second!" Unbeknownst to
Travis, he had already received the third: newly painted
walls in the bedroom where he would soon be sleeping.

Skye looked at the clock. Ten fifteen. She had an
hour and forty-five minutes until Travis arrived to pick
her up. That had to be plenty of time.

The note from Travis said Luna had already been
fed. Skye took her outside briefly and then brought
her back inside. After getting a glass of milk from the
fridge, she quickly downed a square of baked oatmeal
studded with fruit and nuts, then sat down to look at
the list she had compiled the week before.

She went to choice number two. It, too, was out of
stock.

Same with choice number three.

The fourth choice was still available—but only for
back order, and it would not ship until January 28,
which was way too late.

Trying not to panic, Skye looked at Luna, who was
watching her carefully, and started a new search.

Like before, nothing seemed exactly right. So she

kept looking. Finally, an hour and fifteen minutes later, she found what turned out to be even better than the original gift that had been out of stock. She ordered it, paying extra to have it shipped by the morning of the twenty-third.

Then, realizing Travis would be home soon to get her, she rushed upstairs and headed for the shower.

Travis came in to find the downstairs peculiarly quiet. Usually, when Skye was home on her days off, she had music playing or was busy cooking something in the kitchen or doing laundry in the mudroom.

Instead, her breakfast dishes were still on the table, next to her computer tablet. Luna was trotting purposefully down the stairs, her tail—which usually would be wagging wildly at the sight of him—at half-mast.

And then he heard it. From the second floor. The sound of Skye moaning, and…a thud. Then a second anguished cry… Wait! Had she just *thrown* something?

"Skye!" He shouted, rushing up the staircase. Luna galloped ahead, leading the way.

Travis dashed down the hall, aware it was completely silent now, and rounded the banister to her open bedroom door. "What the hell happened?"

It looked like a bomb had exploded in her bedroom.

Cheeks flushed, she was sitting on the still-rumpled covers of her bed, clothes scattered all around her. She had never looked more miserable.

"I can't get a single pair of pants that I own to zip, that's what!"

Relief poured through him. That was all this was?

The wardrobe crisis they probably both should have been expecting?

"You didn't buy any maternity clothes yet?"

She threw up her hands in exasperation. "I haven't needed them."

This was not an unsolvable problem. "Well, we *are* going shopping."

"I'll have to wear yoga pants."

He sat down next to her on the bed and took her in his arms. "You look great in yoga pants."

She buried her face in his shoulder and held on tight. "I'm sorry." Her words were muffled. "I don't know why this is so upsetting to me. I've been incredibly emotional and stressed out all morning."

He threaded his hands through her hair and waited until she looked at him, knowing all he wanted to do was make it better for her. "Do you want to put off the shopping or send me out to do it on my own?"

Skye shook her head, abruptly pulling herself together. She eased away from him. "Not a chance, cowboy." She disappeared into her closet and returned with a flannel shirt in a Christmas plaid that, when buttoned, would hide her baby bump and just skim the top of her thighs. The black yoga pants went on next.

They were…snug.

Too snug for comfort, it appeared. But sexy as hell, nevertheless…

The doorbell rang.

They looked at each other. "Expecting someone?" he asked.

"No." Suddenly, she looked wary. "You?"

He shook his head. "I'll get it." He went down the stairs, with Luna trotting behind him.

Veterinarian and neighboring rancher Sara Anderson-McCabe was at the door. She held a basket with a big red ribbon in her hands. "Hey, Travis! Merry Christmas!"

"Merry Christmas to you!" He ushered her inside. "What is all this?"

"A gift from the vet clinic for fostering this little one." She stood in the foyer, handing the basket over to him.

It contained a nylon chew bone for Luna and low-cal dog treats. As well as hot cocoa mix and a tin of cookies for the humans.

"I also wanted to check in, see how things were going now that you've had this little darling for nearly three weeks," Sara continued.

Skye rushed down the stairs, her feet clad in a pair of moccasins. Her shirt was buttoned one-off all the way down. He looked over the rest of her. Her cheeks were a bright self-conscious pink, her hair tousled from all the pulling on and off of clothes. To their guest, it must have looked as if she had just tumbled out of—or into—bed.

An onslaught of erotic memories hit him.

Oblivious to his thoughts, Sara grinned as if recalling their newlywed status. "Um, but you know, maybe I should have called first. I didn't mean to interrupt anything…"

"You didn't. Well, except maybe a huge wardrobe crisis on my part," Skye said ruefully. "So, what's up?"

Sara continued, "I wanted to find out if you were

set for the holidays or needed help boarding Luna or anything."

Travis lifted his hand. "We're not going to board her."

Skye moved closer to him, as did their beagle. "Luna's spending Christmas with us!" she insisted.

Sara surveyed them all with a pleased look. "So you're still planning to adopt, then?" she affirmed.

"Yes! Absolutely!" Travis and Skye said in unison.

"Would you like to finalize it before the twenty-fifth?" Sara asked.

Skye's eyes filled with happy tears. Her hand flew to her heart. "Could we?" she asked hoarsely.

The vet nodded. "Actually—" she reached into her bag "—I've got the papers right here. All you two have to do is sign on the dotted line."

Minutes later, the door shut, and Sara was headed off to make her next house call.

Travis turned to Skye. "Well, it's official. We are a family of three, soon to be four."

Now all he had to do was figure out a way to get Skye to want to stay a family as much as he did.

Chapter Eighteen

Skye went upstairs to see if she could find a slightly more comfortable pair of pants and caught a reflection of herself in the bedroom mirror. Suddenly, she understood the funny look she had initially gotten from their guest. She turned back to Travis. "I can't believe my shirt was buttoned wrong! And my hair!" She touched a hand to her rumpled strands. Had she even run a brush through them this morning? She couldn't recall. Which meant probably not!

His shoulder rested against the doorframe. He was gazing at her as if she was the most magnificent creature he had ever seen. "You look beautiful."

In his eyes, maybe, Skye thought, embarrassed. Moaning, she put her hand over her face. "No wonder Sara thought she might have come at a bad time."

"Who knows?" Travis straightened and sauntered toward her lazily. He winked at her. "Another fifteen minutes or so, and she *might* have…"

"Very funny, cowboy." Skye shimmied out of her too-tight pants, which were squeezing the breath out of her, and looked down to correctly match her buttons. Travis helped, his fingers brushing against the bare skin of her midriff.

Immediately, her body began to tingle, and her middle took on that hot, melting sensation only he could initiate. "You know we're still going shopping."

Crinkles appeared at the corners of his eyes. "Haven't forgotten. Plus, now we have something even more important to do," he said seriously. "Buy you some maternity clothes."

And just like that, a little of the Christmas magic went out of Skye's day.

Travis wasn't sure what he'd said wrong. Women usually loved to go shopping, didn't they? His sisters had been beyond excited buying maternity clothes.

"Are you worried about the cost?" he asked, perplexed. "Because I've got it."

Skye's face darkened. "No. It's not that," she said in a low, strangled voice. "And you are not going to pay for my clothes, married or not. I've got plenty of earnings for that."

He cupped her shoulders between his palms when he sensed she might bolt. "Then what is it?" he asked. "Because you don't look exactly happy right now." He kissed the nape of her neck, running his hand across the gentle slope of her tummy. "Are you worried about gaining weight or something?"

She inhaled deeply, the action lifting the soft swell of her increasingly full breasts. "No. It's not that. So far, I'm right on track to gain a total of twenty-five pounds. Which is what my obstetrician recommends."

"Then…?" He took her by the hand and guided her over to sit next to him on the side of the bed. "What's got that smile of yours turned upside down?"

For a moment, he didn't think she was going to tell him. He continued to wait. Finally, she tightened her fingers in his, misery written all over her face. "It's what happened the last time."

When she had miscarried.

Her lower lip trembling, she went on to confess, "I was so excited, I rushed right out and bought maternity clothes before I even needed them. And then a few days after that, I lost the baby and ended up having to return nearly everything." Her eyes misted over. "What I had already worn, I donated."

"I'm sorry." He didn't know what else to say. Probably nothing would help. The pain was just going to be there until it wasn't. Or maybe it would always be there; she would just feel it less and less every day.

Determined to be there for her in any case, he asked even more gently, "Are you having any signs that something could possibly be wrong this time, too?"

Fighting tears, Skye pinched the bridge of her nose with her fingertips. "No, that's just it!" She swallowed hard. "It's hard to explain, but I can feel the difference this time." She turned toward him, fiercely maternal now. "I can feel how strong and healthy I am, and how strong and healthy the baby is, too."

He cupped her face in his palm. "And yet you're still scared."

"Not most of the time." She leaned into his touch with a pensive sigh. "But yeah… I guess there is still a part of me that is waiting for the next brick to fall. And that frustrates the heck out of me because the only thing I want to feel now is happy and excited and thrilled to be having your baby."

Ah. Now she was going to make *him* tear up. "Well, I'm thrilled you're having *our* baby," he said gruffly, meaning it from the depths of his heart and soul.

She nodded.

Then she took another deep breath. "Well, then, cowboy, what do you say we put my anxiety aside and go buy a comfy pair of maternity jeans and a shirt or sweater?"

He'd like to buy out the whole damn store if that would make her feel better. But that was apparently not what she wanted. "Starting small?" He got up and moved aside to let her pass.

"Yeah." Skye went back to getting ready to go. She squared her slender shoulders. "I think I just need to prove to myself I can do this, you know?"

He did.

"That my life won't always end in tragedy."

Travis and Luna went back to watching her search for a more comfortable pair of yoga pants. "I'm all on board for that."

* * *

As it turned out, Skye bought two pairs of maternity pants, two button-ups and a pretty turtleneck sweater in a cheerful Christmas red. Travis wouldn't let her leave the maternity boutique until she bought herself a couple pairs of pajamas, too.

Afterward, they went on to finish their Christmas shopping for his family, then stopped by the pet store in San Angelo, where they bought a few more toys and treats for Luna.

They were on the way back to the car with their purchases when they walked past a quilt shop with beautiful baby blankets in the front window. Beyond that was a baby boutique. The displays were equally stunning, especially a soft white outfit that included a matching onesie, cap and blanket, meant for taking the baby home from the hospital.

Travis followed her gaze, his expression gentling. "We're going to need one of those, aren't we?" he said.

Once again, he saw everything she was thinking and feeling. And he knew exactly how to respond to make her feel a whole lot better.

She leaned into him, the fear she had felt earlier almost completely gone. Knowing with him by her side, she could handle anything, she drew a breath and gazed deep into his eyes. "We are."

He studied her. "Want to get it and wrap it up and put it under the tree? Just as a symbolic thing?"

His suggestion was incredibly sentimental. And sweet. Skye didn't know how she had managed to get this far in her life without him. She just knew she didn't want to ever be without him again.

And not just because he was going to be a great dad. But also because he was already a great husband.

She tucked her hand in his. "I think that's a great idea, cowboy. Let's go and get it." Thanks to him, she was ready to start living in the hope and promise of not just this Christmas season but their entire future.

Her heart filling with joy, Skye realized she could not have received a better early Christmas gift. Or married a better man.

Skye had just gotten home from the hospital Thursday evening when she and Travis both received an email from Izzie.

"We could ignore it," he said.

Seeing he had no intention of accessing the message on his phone, Skye got her tablet. No way was she going to wait until morning or later to deal with this. It would drive her too crazy in the meantime if she tried. "When has that worked?" she asked him.

Travis scowled, still looking as unmovable as a two-ton pickup truck. "Never."

It was her turn to be relentlessly courageous. "I know we mutually agreed not to respond to her messages, but let's just look at it," she suggested mildly.

Travis sat beside her. "Wow," he said when the black-and-white photos came up. Clearly taken many years ago, they were of Izzie's husband Kirk's great-granddad's home.

The three-story Victorian was the spitting image of

the ranch house they had inherited from Willa and Walter Braeloch. It had the exact same gabled roof and front door located on one side, with a wraparound porch that went all the way across the front and down one side of the house.

"'Wow' is right. Izzie's done some research," Skye said, scanning the accompanying letter and recapping for Travis. "It turns out the same architectural plan and blueprint was used for both. There were a few minor changes, of course. According to this letter, Kirk's great-granddad had added a room off the back in later years to use as a sunporch that Kirk recalls fondly. And he remembered that house as being painted brown with white trim. But otherwise, it's like his ancestral family home is still here instead of being torn down to make way for a subdivision back in the '80s."

Skye pointed at a section of the letter that Izzie had written for them both to read together. *Now do you see why I want Winding Creek?* Izzie wrote. *Call me tonight! It's not too late to make the kind of deal you both will love!*

Below that, the heiress had written her cell and home numbers. Again. As well as her Realtor's, in case they couldn't get ahold of her.

"You have to hand it to her," Travis said, "the woman is persistent."

Her emotions whirling, Skye frowned. "You'd think with it being so close to Christmas that Izzie would want to be focusing on that instead of this." Just like she and Travis were.

"Maybe she's a last-minute shopper?" Travis joked.

Skye elbowed him lightly in the ribs. "What are we going to do?" She shifted to face him, a foreboding feeling that Izzie was somehow going to say or do something that would ruin everyone's holidays rising within her. "I mean, nothing we've done thus far has worked to discourage her."

"I'll write her. Tell her that although the facts she has uncovered are amazing, our position has not changed. We won't be selling until…" Travis paused, turning his attention back to the screen. "Do you want to say summer at the very earliest?"

Actually, what Skye wanted to say was *never*. They would never sell and instead find a way to stay here, just as Walter and Willa had wanted, and raise their baby together in every sense of the word.

But that was jumping ahead to an ending that might not ever occur—no matter how much she wanted it. She couldn't put that kind of pressure on them.

When she didn't answer, Travis turned back to her. "Is that okay with you?" He squinted. "Or did you have some other timeline in mind?"

Not one she could say. Not without possibly upsetting the very delicate balance of happiness they had found with each other.

"No, it's fine," Skye fibbed.

Travis gave her another long assessing look. Unable to help herself—it was Christmas after all, the time of miracles—she said, "But maybe you should say something like early fall instead." When her maternity leave had ended. "Just so she won't keep asking."

Travis nodded. "I will also suggest, now that she

found the actual blueprint of the ancestral home, that she think about finding some land that is currently for sale and consider building a replica there instead. Although it would likely not be ready for them to actually stay there until summer, it's the thought that counts, and that would still be a hell of a Christmas gift for her husband and kids."

"And a project they could all get involved in." Skye beamed. "Have I told you that you're brilliant?" She leaned over to kiss him.

He kissed her back just as happily. "Like that idea, hmm?"

"I like not having to deal with this," Skye affirmed, watching him type the agreed-upon message on his phone. "So we can concentrate on how much fun we are having getting ready for the holidays."

"Done!" Travis turned off the sound on his phone and put it aside. He set her tablet out of reach, too. "Now… where were we?" he murmured, taking her back into his arms. "Oh, I know—having fun." And in the spirit of the season, they celebrated by making love.

Chapter Nineteen

"Thanks for agreeing to meet with me on such short notice," Travis told his dad on Friday morning.

Robert ushered him inside the Circle L ranch house. "It's no problem. I would have been happy to stop by your place if that were more convenient."

Travis set down his backpack, shrugged out of his winter jacket and hung it on the coatrack. "Skye has the day off."

"So this isn't something you want her to hear," Robert surmised.

"Not yet," he admitted, wishing there were more than four days until Christmas. This was really cutting it close.

Robert led Travis into his study, then settled behind his desk while Travis took a seat in one of the two leather armchairs in front of it. He unzipped the top of his backpack and leaned forward earnestly. "Now that we have a baby on the way, Skye and I have been thinking a lot about our future—and the finances that entails."

Robert rested his forearms on the sides of his chair. "I thought that was pretty much set with what you will each get when you sell Winding Creek next spring."

Travis went ahead and pulled out the folder he had prepared and set it on his lap. "Yeah, well, Dad, that's the thing. I'm not so sure selling is the right thing to do. But we can't afford to stay there indefinitely unless changes are made."

Robert steepled his hands. "You want to run cattle there again?"

"Yes." Travis handed over copies of the business proposal he had brought with him. "But not mine exclusively. I was hoping you might want to lease some land from us and raise a herd there, for at least a few years. That way you could expand your herd—maybe work on developing a new breed of cattle, the way you've been wanting to—and then I'd have enough to pay the taxes and for the upkeep of the property."

"While still keeping your handyman business," Robert assumed.

Travis nodded. He had a lot of local folks depending on him now. "Which I am also hoping to expand." He explained the plan Zach had helped him craft that would involve military veterans fresh out of the service and looking for work.

This impressed his dad.

"Would you help out with the ranching at Winding Creek?" Robert asked.

Travis thought about how much he had always enjoyed working side by side with his dad, even when he'd been burning to follow his own dreams and become a self-made man, too. "I could do that part-time," he said honestly. "But initially, I have to keep my other business going if I want income coming in, so we'd probably have to rely on your hired hands to help out as needed."

Robert flipped through the proposal in front of him, squinting thoughtfully from time to time. "Are you ever going to run your own cattle there?"

"I'd like to."

His dad's expression lit up. "Really?"

"I realized after the winter storm, when I helped out here, how much I missed ranching. So yeah—if I can swing it financially, I'd like to have some of my own herd, too."

"I'm glad to hear that." Robert beamed. "You've always had such a talent for it. What does Skye think about all this?"

Travis tensed. "I haven't told her," he admitted reluctantly, hoping his dad would understand the reasons behind his secrecy. "I wanted to make sure it was even a possibility before I did." There had been no sense raising Skye's hopes only to dash them again.

Robert continued studying the numbers in front of him. "And if I say no?"

Travis felt like he had just been sucker punched. But he kept his manner as mild as possible. "I'll see if

I can find anyone else who wants to lease pastureland from me. At least for a few years."

Robert pushed away from his desk and rocked back in his chair. "A few years is a long time for someone who agreed to stay married for only 120 days."

This was turning into an inquisition. The kind he hadn't had since he was a wayward teenager. Travis stood and began to pace the study restlessly. "That was then, Dad. When we made that agreement with each other, we didn't have a baby on the way—that we knew of, anyway. But now that we do..." He paused to look at the happy Lockhart-family photographs on the shelves. Reminded of what he ultimately wanted, he continued practically, "Well, a baby needs a home. And two loving parents."

"Who love the baby?" Robert asked. "Or love the baby *and* each other?"

The tension in the room grew to an uncomfortable level. "Why are you asking me all these things?" he demanded, feeling hurt despite his determination not to be.

"Because you're asking me to expand my herd beyond what Circle L pastureland can support. That's a long-term proposition of at least two to three years. And your reasoning isn't as solid as I'd like it to be."

"What do you mean?" Travis countered, stung, aware there was nothing more crucial to him than the health and well-being of his new family. "I told you, I am doing this for Skye and the baby and our future."

"But you haven't said anything about love."

When Travis said nothing in return—because there

was nothing he could say on that issue—Robert continued, "Are you and Skye in love with each other? Because nothing has to be settled today or even next spring. The two of you can continue with temporary measures until you are fully ready to commit."

"I'm not sure that will work, Dad. There are taxes and utilities that will have to be paid once the land is ours and the temporary maintenance fund the Braelochs established runs out…"

"I will loan you whatever cash you need for as long as you need to know your own hearts."

Travis hadn't come there asking for a handout; he had wanted a business partnership. The kind his dad had talked about in the past. But seeing that wasn't what Robert wanted to talk about, Travis admitted, "We've already got someone trying to buy the ranch."

Robert paused. "You think Skye wants to sell?"

Travis wished he knew for sure. "Not…necessarily. But she wants a secure financial future. The kind she's never had—and will never have, in terms of money in the bank, unless we do sell and split the proceeds down the middle."

Robert lifted a brow. "So this plan of yours…"

"Is meant to reassure her."

"And you think that's what Skye wants?" his dad asked. "Dollars and cents?"

Was it?

Sometimes when he looked at her, especially before and after they'd made love—or even when they were sitting together in front of the fire at night, with Luna curled at their feet—Skye gazed back at him in a way that seemed to emote love. Real romantic love. The kind good, enduring marriages were built on.

But she'd never said as much.

And he'd made a heartbreaking error once before, romantically mistaking a business partnership for more.

Only to get dumped in the end.

Travis resumed his pacing. "I don't know what Skye feels, Dad. Except that she needs and wants security. For her and the baby." Travis stood, legs braced apart, arms folded. "And I am bound and determined to give her that."

"That's admirable."

He dropped his arms, aware he was practically pleading now, which was something he never did. "So you'll help me?"

Robert promised stalwartly, "I'll give it very serious consideration."

That, unfortunately, was not the same as a yes.

Disappointment flowed through Travis. He had never wanted to go to his dad, hat in hand; had never wanted to depend on anyone or anything.

"But I can't say yes," Robert concluded, "until I am sure that you *and Skye* are both in this for all the right reasons, for more than just a few more months."

As Skye had hoped, the UPS truck came while Travis was gone for the day.

"Oh my gosh! This is just perfect!" she said to Luna as she hurriedly carted the packages upstairs and un-wrapped the second gift for Travis. "The blue-gray linens we ordered online are the perfect match! And I love the pillows. They are so soft and fluffy!"

The question was, had she gone overboard? Especially considering the fact that the biggest present of all was not even going to be delivered until the following day, the morning of the twenty-third?

She turned back to Luna, who sat beside her, watching happily. Suddenly, the beagle stood up and turned toward the window. Skye turned in the direction of her canine companion. With a sinking heart, she saw a sleek black town car coming up the drive. It stopped in front of the ranch house, and a uniformed driver got out and walked around to open the back door. Izzie stepped out. She was dressed in a long black wool coat and boots. Sunglasses shaded her eyes.

"Unbelievable!" Skye bit out. Then, with a resigned sigh, she headed down the hall with Luna trotting happily at her side. "I guess we better go see what she wants this time."

The doorbell was ringing by the time they reached the foyer. Skye went to answer the door, reminding herself this was indeed Christmas, the season of charity. She forced herself to greet her as warmly as she could. "Izzie! What a surprise!"

The heiress kept her dark glasses on. Her manner was remarkably subdued. "May I come in?"

Nodding graciously, Skye stepped back and asked, "Would your chauffeur like to come in, too?"

"Oh, heavens no!" Izzie breezed past in a cloud of what almost smelled like cigarette smoke covered up with expensive perfume. "He's used to waiting on me."

Well, okay, then! Nodding, Skye shut the door.

Izzie handed off her coat as if Skye were the coat check person in a fancy restaurant. Then she walked into the living room and looked around, taking a seat in the wingback chair adjacent to the lit Christmas tree.

"Can I get you something to drink?"

"No. Thanks." Izzie pushed her dark glasses up on top of her head.

Skye was shocked to see the heiress's eyes were red and puffy, as if she had been crying a good long time. "I got your husband's response to my latest offer," the woman reported unhappily.

"This isn't personal, Izzie. Travis and I can't sell the property until we have resided here for at least 120 days, which will be in April. It's part of the terms of our inheritance."

"You're sure there is no way around it? I've got lawyers who can work miracles with any contract."

Skye shook her head. "It's more than that. We're fulfilling the Braelochs' last wish. We can't renege on that."

Izzie tapped her fingers impatiently. "Well, what if we were to sign a contract now that won't close until mid-April? We could go ahead and agree on the amount, and I could wire the two of you a substantial down payment today. The transaction itself would still be in all cash. All inspections and repairs waived. Would you consider it then?"

Would she?

All Skye could really think was this had become

their home. The place Luna loved. The ranch where she wanted to raise their child.

"Look, I understand that the architecture of this home is an exact replica of Kirk's great-grandad's home. But as you've pointed out on more than one occasion, this place is 110 years old. Wouldn't it be better to just buy some land and build a new home, in this exact style, there? That could have all the comforts you-all are accustomed to?"

Izzie began to cry. "That'll be too late!" Her shoulders shook with the force of her sobs. "This gift is probably the only thing that will keep Kirk from divorcing me!"

Divorcing? "You're separated?" Skye asked.

"No. Not yet." Izzie sniffed. "But I overheard him talking on the phone just before Thanksgiving. He said he planned to make it through the holidays for the kids' sake but that was it, as far as he was concerned. He was going to put an end to our travesty of a marriage." She cried harder.

No wonder she'd been so desperate. Skye pulled up an ottoman and sat down in front of the distraught woman. Her experience as a registered nurse, dealing with people in crisis, came to the fore. "Have you talked to Kirk about any of this?" she asked gently.

Izzie shook her head emphatically as the tears continued to roll. "I know he married me for all the wrong reasons."

Skye paused, confused.

"I was pregnant. And we had only been dating a

short while, but my parents insisted we marry and do what was best for the baby. At least for a while."

This has a too-familiar ring to it, Skye thought uncomfortably. Although the decision to stay married for the baby's sake, at least for a while, had been hers and Travis's.

Izzie stroked the large diamond on her left hand. "To help us get started, my dad gifted us our home in River Oaks. He also gave Kirk a fast-track job at Wheaton Oil."

Skye got a box of tissues and handed it over. "Does he still work there?"

"Yes." Izzie pulled out a tissue and blew her nose. "But Kirk's never really been comfortable with the lifestyle of my family, even though he's now been very high up in the executive ranks for the last ten years."

"Which is why you want Winding Creek," Skye supposed.

Izzie nodded. "He thinks I don't really 'get' him or where he's from. That I don't do nearly enough for him or the kids. Don't you see, Skye?" Izzie asked, her steely determination coming through. "I've got to prove my devotion to him and the kids once and for all. Or my family will be wrecked forever!"

Travis was still smarting from the meeting with his dad when he pulled up behind the black town car parked in front of the Winding Creek ranch house.

Somehow, he wasn't surprised to see Izzie walk out of the house, Skye and Luna next to her. What was so astonishing was the fact that the two women were so deep in conversation, they didn't notice his truck.

What the hell?

Travis watched them hug; then Izzie put on her dark glasses and hurried down the porch steps to the town car. Her driver opened the door for her.

Already feeling like he had been kicked in the gut by the disappointing talk with his dad, he watched the town car depart, then got out. Leaving his backpack in the truck, he walked slowly up to the porch, where a shivering Skye and Luna stood.

"Did I miss something?" he asked, not sure he could take any more disappointment that day.

Apparently so, judging by the reluctant expression on Skye's pretty face. "Let's get in out of the cold." She took his arm and guided him inside.

Luna followed happily, heading for the hearth. He saw legal documents strewn across the coffee table.

Another stab of anxiety twisted his gut. "What's all this?" And why had Skye met with the heiress without including him in the meeting?

She took his coat and led him over to the sofa, where they sat down, side by side. "Izzie brought another offer. For 2.5 million this time."

He glanced over at the reams of official-looking documents and contracts before turning back to Skye. "The ranch is only valued at two million."

"Technically, yes, but to Izzie, it is worth a lot more. And since she is not applying for a mortgage, she can pay us whatever she wants to pay us for the property." Skye blew out a breath. "Anyway, she is proposing that we live here until mid-April and close the deal then, after you and I have completed our 120-day stay here. We wouldn't have to vacate the property until then. We would just need to agree to let her husband and children in on the surprise and briefly tour the property on Christmas Day before they head to Aspen for the New Year."

Travis felt like he had entered an alternate universe. "You're seriously considering this?"

Skye waved her hands vaguely. For a second, she looked torn, like she didn't know what she wanted to do. Then she released a breath and said, "Izzie told me that her husband is going to leave her." She went on to explain further while he listened in disbelief. "Izzie thinks closing this deal is the only way she will be able to keep her family intact."

Travis could see the spoiled heiress had somehow made Skye believe this was their problem to solve, not hers! He got to his feet, growling, "I hate to tell you this, but money is and has never been the path to happiness. Izzie is living proof of that."

Skye studied him cautiously. "So you don't think we should say yes?"

He blinked. "*Do you?*"

"I don't know!" she retorted, clearly conflicted. She rose to her feet, too, squaring off with him. "It would mean an extra quarter of a million dollars for both of us. That would pay for our child's college education and, if invested wisely, anything else he or she will need growing up."

He appreciated her playing devil's advocate so they

could see both sides of the issue. Still… "We could do that without selling Winding Creek, Skye."

"I don't see how," she reminded him, "when you've already said you don't want to turn this into a working ranch."

Too late, he saw he should have shared his thoughts on that with her a whole lot earlier. "I would do that to stay," he vowed.

Adamantly, she vetoed the suggestion. "Don't you see? I don't want you to do something you have never felt you were suited for. Trust me, that never works out. I learned that the hard way."

Another punch, right in the ribs. "You're talking about your former fiancé?"

"Dex never wanted to have kids. But he stepped up when I was pregnant and was secretly miserable. Had I not lost the baby, then he would have gone on to marry me out of duty and responsibility. And then we probably would have ended up where Izzie Wheaton and her husband Kirk are right now."

"So you're comparing me to your *ex*?" He couldn't believe this! "And Izzie's miserably married spouse?" What had he done—or *not* done—to deserve this?

Skye shook her head sadly. "I'm saying I don't want to end up in that situation. Not again." Her voice cracked. "I don't want a baby or money or even this ranch to be the thing that keeps us together, Travis."

"Because you don't love me," he presumed brokenly, feeling like everything he thought they had together had just been unceremoniously yanked away from him.

"I…" She started to say something else but stopped.

Tears flooded her eyes. Finally, she managed to pull herself together. "Solid marriages need love for a foundation, Travis." She inhaled deeply. "If I have learned anything today, it is that."

He threw up his hands in disgust that it had come to this, and he clenched his jaw. "Well, then, that makes two of us," he said in a voice that sounded defeated, even to him. Knowing he had to get away before they said anything else hurtful to each other, he spun away from her.

She moved to block his path, her pretty eyes wide with surprise. "Wait! Where are you going?"

"I don't know."

She lifted a delicate palm in stop sign fashion. "Travis, Izzie needs a response within two hours!"

He turned away, so sick of being used and misled. "Then tell her yes," he barked, sure now that was what Skye really wanted. Lots of money in hand and the security that came with it. "We agree to her latest offer," he continued, giving up the fight. Skye'd made it clear: there was no future for them. Not as husband and wife, anyway. So what was the point? "We'll sell."

Skye looked at him as if she wanted everything to be crystal clear. "What about our vow to honor Walter and Willa's last wish?"

Finding it ironic that she would care more about the deceased couple's wishes and Izzie and Kirk Wheaton's failing marriage than their own, he countered, "We can still abide by the terms of the will and make good on our promise by having one meal a day together and sleeping under the same roof every night. For at least another ninety-plus days."

Luna came up to them, her tail low and barely moving, her expression dejected—as if she were wondering where she fit in all of this.

"And then?" Skye demanded, looking stricken.

Funny. That was exactly how *he* felt. He knelt down to pet the dog they had quickly come to love and just mutually adopted. He shrugged and forced himself to be as coolly practical as he needed to be under the circumstances. "We'll split the money from the sale, find new places to live and figure out where we go from there."

Chapter Twenty

"I figured I would find you here," Robert Lockhart said from the doorway of Callahan Custom Carpentry early on the morning of December 23.

Travis looked up from the kitchen island he had built. The butcher block top already had three good coats of polymerizing oil on it, but he had decided last night to add another and was now buffing the top to perfection.

Robert ambled closer. "Your mom stopped by Winding Creek this morning on her way to work, and you weren't there."

Travis shrugged, still feeling a little stiff and tired from the sleepless night in the guest room. He didn't know how he and Skye were going to manage another three months under the same roof every night. "I guess I had already left," he said.

Which wasn't surprising, since he had gotten up before dawn in order to avoid running into Skye. And then only stayed long enough to take care of a sad-looking Luna before he left.

Robert removed his Stetson and shearling coat, and hung each on one of the hooks that were in a row next to the door. Expression grim, he ambled closer, pausing to search his son's face. "Skye said she wasn't going to be at Christmas dinner at the Circle L. She wasn't sure what your plans were." His brow furrowed. "What's going on?"

Nothing I wish were happening, that's for damn sure. Travis inhaled, bracing himself for whatever parental advice was to come. He looked his dad in the eye, speaking man-to-man, "We got an offer for the ranch." Briefly, he explained Izzie Wheaton's visit and the depth of the heiress's predicament.

Robert nodded as he listened. "I'm guessing Skye's heart went out to her?"

Was that what had happened? Or was this the easy out his wife had been looking for all along? Travis was unsure. Still buffing the island top, he confided what he knew for sure. "Up to then, everything Izzie had done seemed like a manipulation. A ruse to get her way. So it was easy to turn her down."

"But not when it came to a matter of the heart," Robert supposed, going over to the beverage station set up against the back wall and helping himself to the workshop coffee.

Finished, Travis went over to join his dad. "Well, you know Skye. She has a heart as big as all Texas." He poured himself a cup of the coffee, too. He had made it several hours earlier, and it was now strong and bitter-tasting. He drank it anyway.

Robert pulled up a stool and sat down. "Except for you?"

His dad's mildly provoking tone rankled him. "What would make you say that?" Travis asked with a frown.

"Well, it seems to be what you're thinking. That she's taken everyone into her heart except you."

Okay, that stings. Trying to ignore the sudden ache in his chest, Travis said, "I think she cares about me, Dad."

Robert presumed, "But not with the unconditional love she gives Luna, for example, or this baby the two of you are going to have?"

Was Skye's affection fleeting? The hurt part of him thought so, but the more reasonable side was not as convinced of anything at this point. All he knew was his own feelings, which were apparently not matched by hers.

"I gather Skye didn't like the plans you had to bring the ranch all the way back to life?"

Travis walked over to the artificial Christmas tree in the corner. It bore all the holiday cheer he no longer felt. He turned back to his dad and, aware Robert was still waiting for an answer, reluctantly admitted, "I never told her."

Robert did a double take and set his mug down with a thud. *"Nothing?"*

Travis's defenses prickled. What had there been to say? "You said no," he reminded his dad.

Robert marched closer. "When has that ever stopped you?" he echoed in obvious frustration. "And I didn't say no. I said for me to commit, it had to be because you and Skye were both on board with the plan for all the right reasons."

Travis sighed. Yet another impossible hurdle for him to clear before he could have even part of what he wanted and needed in this life. "Meaning we were head over heels in love."

The grooves on either side of Robert's mouth deepened. "Aren't you?"

"Look, Dad, as much as I would rather not admit it, Skye had the right idea."

"About what?" his father asked.

Travis blew out a resigned breath. "About legally putting the ranch under contract now, accepting a tidy sum of earnest money and locking in the price, so we could sell to Izzie in the spring once we had met the 120-day marriage terms of the inheritance."

"Even if selling out isn't what you want or think is best for your growing family?"

"I know it's not what everyone—" *including me* "—was hoping would happen… But Skye and I need to be smart about this and not get caught up in the excitement and emotion of the holidays and the baby on the way. We need to go back to our original agreement, honorably follow the terms of the will and then come to an amicable legal end—while still raising our child together, of course."

"So…" Robert went back to the beverage station to pour himself another mug of the terrible coffee. "You're back to letting money rule your life again."

Didn't everything always come back to that in the end? His biological parents' death? His breakup with Alicia and now Skye? Money was always at the heart of every tragedy and heartache he had suffered to date. "I don't want the money from the inheritance, Dad. I never did."

"But you're not willing to turn it down entirely," Robert presumed, "so you can't fight for what you really want, either."

"Skye and I had an agreement."

His father countered sagely, "One that seems to have changed over time."

Yes, it had. And in the end, not for the better, it appeared. "That's the thing about being impulsive, Dad. It never works out in the long haul."

Robert closed the distance between them. Clapping him affectionately on the shoulder, in the way fathers comforted their offspring, he murmured, "Not necessarily, son. All I know for sure is that following your heart and going after love with all you've got—*that* is going to bring you the kind of soul-deep happiness your mother and I have always wanted for you."

A little while later, Skye stood on the front porch, signing the receipt the two delivery men had for her.

The driver of the truck peered at her from beneath his cap, taking in the tears still rolling down her face.

"I know we already put it inside, but you don't have to accept delivery if this really isn't what you want."

Aware she must appear ridiculous, she cried harder. "That's the problem," she said, sniffing. "It is exactly the gift I wanted!"

Unpersuaded, the driver said, "I know it's the twenty-third, but we'll still be out making deliveries till noon tomorrow. So we could probably fix whatever is wrong… It's really not too late."

Wasn't it? The way Travis had looked at her before he had walked out, the way he had completely avoided her in the nearly twenty hours since, said it was. Skye swallowed another wave of tears. "That's very kind of you. But it's way too late to fix what's really broken. And for the record, it's really not what you put upstairs for me. That is every bit as wonderful as I expected it to be."

"Well, that's good to hear." The driver nodded at his companion, who went around and climbed in the passenger side of the truck. "As for the other…whatever it is, try not to give up hope. It is Christmas, after all!"

She knew. Wow, did she ever know. It was part of what was shattering her heart, how high her hopes had been this entire last month. "Thank you for all your help," she told the driver.

He tipped the brim of his hat, nodded and walked away. He was just driving off as Emma Lockhart drove up. The truck driver stopped and rolled down his window. Travis's sister rolled down hers. Skye could see them saying something to each other, which had Emma nodding in the end.

Somehow, Skye wasn't surprised to see Travis's little sister and closest sibling somehow inject herself in the middle of her and Travis's troubles—any more than she had been to see Carol stop by that morning.

The Lockharts had a sixth sense when it came to the well-being of their family members. And there was no disputing it: she and Travis were in the ditch. At least when it came to their relationship.

Emma parked and marched up to the porch, looking deeply concerned. As usual, she cut straight to the chase. "You want to tell me what is going on?" she asked kindly. "And it's not just those two delivery people who are concerned or think you may be in need of some sort of family assistance! I've just come from talking to Travis. My dad was there earlier. Neither of us have ever seen him so sad in his life!"

"'Sad'?" A tiny flicker of hope flared inside her. *Is it possible that Travis is just as broken up as I am about what happened?*

"Okay." Emma sighed, relenting, and said in a slightly more practical tone, "Well, maybe he was a little angry and discouraged, too."

That, Skye could have expected since she felt the same. Unfortunately, it was about to get worse.

Clearly eager to help, the other woman pressed, "So what is going on, Skye?"

So much more than even Travis knows right now. Shivering in the cold, Skye ushered her inside, closing the door behind them. "I didn't follow our agreement to deal with everything about the ranch together, as equals."

Emma looked over at the unlit Christmas tree and the stockings that still lined the mantel. "And he found out?"

Skye went to turn up the thermostat in the front hall. "No. I don't think he knows yet," she admitted sourly. "Otherwise, he probably would have at least texted me or sent me a message through a third party or something."

Travis's sister shrugged out of her coat and hung it over the end of the banister, still struggling to understand. She sat down on the bottom stairs and, seeing Luna, motioned for the beagle to come closer. Luna did and was rewarded with affectionate petting from another dog-loving Lockhart. "So that's why you've obviously been crying? Because you're dreading Travis's reaction to what you did?"

It is certainly part of it. "Yes."

Emma made a dissenting face as she snuggled Luna all the more. "Travis doesn't have a temper, Skye."

He didn't have *any* bad qualities, as far as Skye was concerned. "I know that. But when he eventually gets here today, he's going to be expecting something to have happened yesterday. And I will have to tell him that I didn't honor his wishes."

Emma shook her head as if that would clear it, complaining, "None of this is making any sense."

"I know. Believe me, I know." Skye shoved her hand through her hair.

The shoe designer gave Luna a final pet, then stood and moved closer to Skye. "This is what I do know. Travis is unhappy. You are clearly just as miserable.

And the only time I've ever seen the two of you even the slightest bit at odds is when you aren't communicating the way a happily married couple should."

Skye sighed. She was so emotionally exhausted. Beyond distraught. "What's your point?" she asked Travis's sister.

"The delivery driver that just left was right. There is always time to set things right if you want something bad enough."

Five hours later, Skye turned to Luna—who had been by her side nonstop both before and after she had stopped crying—and said, as she skidded to a halt in front of their lit, beautifully decorated Christmas tree, "Oh, Luna, I have to get this right. I just am not sure what I should say."

The dog looked at her intently with her big dark eyes. She seemed to be telling Skye to go for it. So she texted,

I know we fought yesterday and didn't speak last night, when you finally came home and went straight to your room and shut the door. But we're still married, Travis. We still have a baby on the way—

Wrong.

The last thing they needed at this point was for either of them to be coerced into anything. If he were going to be here with her and Luna, he needed to want to be here.

She deleted what she'd written. "The truth is, mistakes were made," Skye admitted with a breadth and depth of honesty that brought relief. "Especially by me." She sighed and continued talking to Luna, taking strength from the dog's quiet wisdom and unconditional, unwavering love and devotion. "Maybe I should just keep it simple."

Her pet's eyes lit up in the equivalent of a doggy smile.

She typed again:

We need to talk.

"We sure do," Travis drawled, coming in through the front door, cell phone in hand.

Skye blinked, hardly able to believe her eyes. Was this a Christmas miracle or what? "You're here!" she cried out with joy, forgetting for a moment they were still supposed to be upset with each other.

Travis nodded emphatically. "I am." He strode toward her, clearly a man on a mission. Wasting no time, he took her in his arms and gave her a long, fiercely loving hug. His words were muffled against her hair, making them no less emotional as he said, "I want to apologize for yesterday."

Skye clung to him, too. "No. It was my fault!"

He inhaled sharply and drew back just enough so she could see the regret etched in the handsome lines of his face. "I should never have told you to sell to Izzie."

The world around them skittered to a stop. Here it was. Her big chance to set the record straight.

Drawing on all her courage, Skye lifted her chin and prepared to fess up to the husband she hoped would be hers for all time. Even after this. She swallowed hard, admitting in a stubbornly defiant tone, "I didn't."

He blinked. *"What?"*

Skye met his searching glance. "When you left, I knew what you wanted, or said you wanted." She rushed on, "But when I went to call Izzie to accept the offer, I realized it wasn't what I wanted or what our baby needed. And although I knew there would be other chances to sell, there might not be other chances to stay and really try and work things out." She drew a quavering breath, then went on, "So I told Izzie that I hoped she and Kirk could work things out for their family's sake but that she couldn't build *her* family's happiness on the destruction of *our* family's happiness."

Travis had gone completely still. "What did she say?" he asked, his expression inscrutable.

Oh, so much, Skye recalled. All of which, unfortunately, Luna had overheard since Skye had tired of the screeching and put the irate woman on speakerphone.

Figuring they could go into the tirade more deeply later, if Travis wanted, Skye kept her recollection brief. "As you can imagine, Izzie wasn't happy, and she made it abundantly clear."

Travis chuckled, as if imagining the spoiled heiress fully revealing herself at long last.

"Suffice it to say that was her best and final offer, and she won't be coming back. So," she concluded on another deep breath, "I hope you're not too mad I just cost us each a quarter of a million dollars."

"Are you kidding?" He took her all the way into his

arms and held her close once again. "I love that you did what you did yesterday."

Which wasn't quite the same as loving her, Skye thought, clinging to him, too. But she had promised herself that she would open up her heart and give it her all, so...

Here went everything!

"Even though you told me to do the opposite?" she asked, wanting to make sure her going rogue really was okay.

"I am especially happy you did that," he told her, looking her in the eye.

"How come?" she asked softly.

"Because my need to keep myself from relying too much on anyone or anything was getting in the way of us getting what we both really wanted." His voice lowered solemnly. "Which was a future with each other."

They were partway to where they needed to be, Skye thought, advising herself to be as patient with him as he needed her to be.

But if this were ever really going to work out long-term, she also had to be scrupulously honest. Clear up all misconceptions and tell him what was really in her heart.

She took him by the hand and led him over to the sofa. As they sat down, Luna settled on the floor in front of them. "I know I told you that financial security was of paramount importance to me and—in the beginning, anyway, because I no longer had any family of my own—money did equal security for me. But deep down, money was never what I wanted from our arrangement,

Travis." She gathered her courage. "I wanted family and the unconditional love that comes with that."

That was the security that mattered. She knew now.

And if she had to settle for just that, she would. Because even if romantic love was the ideal, love was still love. And since she and Travis loved each other as friends and co-parents and lovers, even more love could grow between them over time. So there was that.

And gauging by the deeply affectionate way he was looking at her, he seemed to agree.

"Well, you've got that now from the entire Lockhart clan," he told her firmly. "And you and I and our child will always have it." He took her hands in his. "Just as you will always be financially taken care of, even without us having to sell the ranch."

It was her turn to be surprised.

She listened as he told her about the business deal he had made with his dad to turn the Winding Creek back into a working cattle ranch that would pay for itself while he continued building up the handyman business he had started.

She sat back, impressed. "Two jobs is a lot."

He shrugged off the prospect of all that hard labor. "You know how I like variety when it comes to my work. As far as the ranch goes, it's time it was brought back to life, to continue on as Walter and Willa always wanted—with a new generation."

Happily, she reflected. "I think they'd like that."

Travis nodded, incredibly serious again. "They'd probably like what I'm about to say to you even better." He tightened his grip on her hands. "I know we entered into this match as two people who barely knew each other, then became friends and then lovers."

His dark brow furrowed.

"And we were supposed to leave it there and keep it simple and uncomplicated so we could co-parent peacefully, but—" he stood and pulled her to her feet "—I can't just leave it at that." He threaded his hands through her hair and tilted her face up to his. "Skye, I love you," he told her huskily. "I love you with all my heart and soul."

Tears blurred her vision. "Oh, Travis, I love you, too!" she told him joyfully. Their lips met in a soft and searing kiss.

They were breathless when they finally stopped. "So about this 120-day marriage of ours…" Travis began.

"First and most importantly," Skye interrupted fiercely, "we need to take the 120-day moniker off of it."

His grin spread. "I agree. *Forever* is what we need. And to prove that to you…" He reached into his pocket and pulled out a small jewelry box. "Your Christmas present. Well, one of them."

"Oh, Travis…" With trembling fingers, she opened it. Saw a dazzlingly beautiful gold band studded with diamonds. Her heart, already full to bursting, expanded all the more to let him in.

"It's an eternity ring," Travis told her hoarsely. "Because that's what I want with you—an eternity."

Tears of happiness flowed.

He helped her put it on next to her wedding band. It fit perfectly.

"It's beautiful. I love it!" she said, hugging him close. "And speaking of presents…" She took him by the hand and led him up the staircase, down to the far end of the upstairs hall. Luna followed close behind. Practically bursting with excitement and the need to give to him spectacularly, too, she said, "I want to show you my gift to you!"

She swung open the door. Dominating the previously empty master suite was a king-size bed with a mahogany headboard and matching nightstand and bureau. The bed had been perfectly made up with the linens and comfy pillows she had spent so much time picking out.

"Wow." He sat down on the edge of the bed, testing the mattress. "This is awesome." He turned to her with a smile of sexual mischief that quickly had her insides revving. "But I think it's too big for just me."

She winked at him playfully. "I thought you might say that."

"So, if I were to give you an invitation to forget the separate bedrooms and move in here with me permanently…?"

Skye headed straight for his strong arms. "I would absolutely accept!"

They spent the next hour making up and making love. As dusk settled over them, Travis glanced at his watch. "Oh, man, we need to get dressed!" he said, reaching for his clothes.

Skye sat up and followed suit. "What's going on?"

"Your next present will be arriving shortly."

Next present? What else could she possibly need? "Something else?"

"Hey. You got me a new and improved bedroom set and new linens, and are joining me here forever more! Of course I got you something else, too. And you're going to love it when you see it," he promised, just as a Callahan Custom Carpentry truck pulled up and Zach and Cade got out.

Luna, who had gone downstairs earlier, came back up to let out a short, urgent bark to tell them they had company. "Good girl, Luna!" he praised her doggy alarm. "Not to worry. I've got it."

Travis finished shoving his feet into his boots, then put his hands on Skye's shoulders. "No peeking, okay? You have to stay here with Luna until I tell you it's okay to come downstairs."

Her excitement escalating, she sat on the edge of the bed, making sure her shirt was correctly buttoned this time. "Whatever you say, cowboy."

A lot of tromping and calling out in deep male voices followed. Finally, Skye was given the all clear signal. She and Luna headed downstairs.

The men were gathered in the kitchen, watching her reaction. At first, she wasn't sure why; then she looked in the center of the room and saw the most beautiful island, with cabinets on one side, a seating area on the other and a large butcher block top. The bottom half had been painted the same serene sage green she and Willa had picked out for the kitchen cabinets. "Oh, Travis…" She couldn't resist touching it.

"It took him weeks to make it," Cade bragged.

"And he did all the work himself," Zach added, "when he easily could have just commissioned it."

Skye turned back to Travis. Talk about a symbol of utter devotion! They really had been thinking of each other's happiness when it came to gift-giving. She wreathed her arms around his neck, so pleased and touched, she could barely speak. "I love it!"

Travis's grin spread even wider. "Glad to hear it, darlin'." His voice was a throaty rumble.

The kind he used when he wanted to make love.

Cade winked at Zach, correctly reading the signs. "Looks like our work is done here," he said as Travis maneuvered Skye beneath a sprig of newly hung mistletoe and lowered his head to give her a soft and celebratory kiss.

"Yeah. Don't mind us," Zach teased. "Just go right on kissing!"

So they did.

Epilogue

One year later...

Travis paced the front hall and looked around at the stacks of things waiting to be carried out to his quad cab while he contentedly cuddled their seven-month-old son, Robbie, against his chest.

Watching, Skye couldn't help but note what a handsome pair the two made. Their infant son had her dark brown hair, his daddy's strong profile, eyes that were starting to be more brown than blue and a sunny personality that constantly filled Travis and Skye with joy. He was completely adored by both of them as well as everyone else in the big and loving Lockhart clan.

"I think we forgot something," Travis drawled.

Skye furrowed her brow, not sure how that could be.

She'd made a very thorough list! "What?" she asked, perplexed.

"The kitchen sink."

Skye shot a comically admonishing look at her husband. "Very funny, cowboy." She stepped around the stack of presents waiting to be carried out, consulted her checklist and added four diapers to the diaper bag. "You better be careful," she teased back with a flirtatious look, aware their love life got hotter and more satisfying with every day that passed. "Or I might just add that to the list."

He grinned, countering, "But that would make us late."

Skye wasn't about to make them late. She enjoyed these family gatherings too much to miss even a second of them. Sobering, she propped her hands on her waist and said, "I'm almost ready. Promise. Just a few more things…"

She headed back to the kitchen, bag in hand, adding several bottles of prepared formula, an infant-sized spoon and a couple of jars of baby food.

Travis followed lazily, turning Robbie around in his arms so their son could watch her, too. "You know, I think my mom has most of these things at the Circle L." He watched as she added a few teething biscuits and a pacifier.

"She's also having everyone over for Christmas dinner this afternoon, which means she's bound to run out of something if we all don't come prepared. Luckily for us, the women in this family have superior managerial skills when it comes to organizing a big holiday get-together."

His glance traveled over her appreciatively. "That, you do. But don't discount the men's involvement."

He was right. The guys were absolutely essential when it came to keeping the fire going and the turkeys and hams cooking on the outdoor grills so the indoor ovens could be used for the side dishes. "Believe me, I'm not! You-all do a wonderful job with your share of the chores and supervision of the kids."

"Hear that, Robbie? She thinks the men in the Lockhart gang are admirable!"

"Especially the two standing right in front of me." She lovingly kissed them both.

Travis grinned and Robbie waved his arms happily.

"Okay." Skye checked off the last item on their list. "We're ready to go. All we have to do is get Robbie's jacket and cap on, and we'll be on our way. Right, Luna?"

Their dog, who had been waiting patiently, thumped her tail.

Travis held their son while she worked on the baby outerwear and put on her own coat as well.

"Why don't you-all stay here while I load the truck," he said.

Luckily, what had taken her a good half an hour to put together took him less than five minutes to get in the cab. Luna—wearing a red tartan collar—went in first, wagging as Travis connected her safety harness to the seat belt. Robbie went in next, cooing softly as they buckled him in his carrier.

Finally, it was time for Travis to gallantly assist Skye up into the cab. "You know, you don't have to keep doing that," she murmured, looking into his eyes.

"It's my pleasure," he retorted in a low, rumbling voice that sent havoc running through her. "Besides—" he bent lower to kiss her gently "—don't you know by now how much I love taking care of all of you?"

Oh, she did.

It was hard not to, given how hard he worked in partnership with his father, turning the Winding Creek back into a cattle ranch while training returning military vets and building up his handyman business.

He'd also been supportive when she had wanted to go back to nursing one day a week, for now, with a more ambitious schedule to come later. Plus, he was always there to lend a hand with Robbie and Luna or anything she needed him to do.

Of course, she spoiled him as well.

Making sure there was nothing he wanted for on a daily basis. And there was not a doubt in her mind that Travis knew how devoted she was to him, too.

She cupped his face in her hands and kissed him back—sweetly, tenderly, aware each day with him seemed to get impossibly better and more joyous. "I love you, cowboy," she murmured against his lips.

"I love you, too." He kissed her one last time.

From the back seat, Robbie chortled louder. Luna let out a happy yip.

Travis chuckled and let her go. "You know what that means, don't you?" He closed the door and circled around to the driver's side.

Skye watched him climb in behind the wheel, in complete husband-and-daddy mode, and nodded. "It's time to get this Lockhart family Christmas show of ours on the road."

* * * * *

COMING NEXT MONTH FROM

HARLEQUIN®
SPECIAL EDITION™

#2953 A FORTUNE'S WINDFALL
The Fortunes of Texas: Hitting the Jackpot • by Michelle Major
When Linc Maloney inherits a fortune, he throws caution to the wind and vows to live life like there's no tomorrow. His friend and former coworker Remi Reynolds thinks that Linc is out of control and tries to remind him that money can't buy happiness. She can't admit to herself that she's been feeling more than *like* for Linc for a long time but doesn't dare risk her heart on a man with a big-as-Texas fear of commitment...

#2954 HER BEST FRIEND'S BABY
Sierra's Web • by Tara Taylor Quinn
Child psychiatrist Megan Latimer would trust family attorney Daniel Tremaine with her life—but never her heart. Danny's far too attractive for any woman's good...until one night changes everything. As if crossing the line weren't cataclysmic enough, Megan and Danny just went from besties and colleagues to parents-to-be. As they work together to resolve a complex custody case, can they save a family and find their own happily-ever-after?

#2955 FALLING FOR HIS FAKE GIRLFRIEND
Sutton's Place • by Shannon Stacey
Over-the-top Molly Cyrs hardly seems a match for bookish Callan Avery. But when Molly suggests they pose as a couple to assuage Stonefield's anxiety about its new male librarian, his pretend paramour is all Callan can think about. Callan's looking for a family, though, and kids aren't in Molly's story. Unless he can convince Molly that she's not "too much"...and that to him, she's just enough!

#2956 THE BOOKSTORE'S SECRET
Home to Oak Hollow • by Makenna Lee
Aspiring pastry chef Nicole Evans is just waiting to hear about her dream job, and in the meantime, she goes to work in the café at the local bookstore. But that's before the recently widowed Nicole meets her temporary boss: her first crush, Liam Mendez! Will his simmering attraction to Nicole be just one more thing to hide...or the stuff of his bookstore's romance novels?

#2957 THEIR SWEET COASTAL REUNION
Sisters of Christmas Bay • by Kaylie Newell
When Kyla Beckett returns to Christmas Bay to help her foster mom, the last person she wants to run into is Ben Martinez. The small-town police chief just wants a second chance—to explain. But when Ben's little girl bonds with his longtime frenemy, he wonders if it might be the start of a friendship. Can the wounded single dad convince Kyla he's always wanted the best for her...then, now and forever?

#2958 A HERO AND HIS DOG
Small-Town Sweethearts • by Carrie Nichols
Former Special Forces soldier Mitch Sawicki's mission is simple: find the dog who survived the explosion that ended Mitch's military career. Vermont farmer Aurora Walsh thinks Mitch is the extra pair of hands she desperately needs. Her young daughter sees Mitch as a welcome addition to their family, whose newest member is the three-legged Sarge. Can another wounded warrior find a home with a pint-size princess and her irresistible mother?

YOU CAN FIND MORE INFORMATION ON UPCOMING HARLEQUIN TITLES, FREE EXCERPTS AND MORE AT HARLEQUIN.COM.

HSECNM1122

HARLEQUIN
PLUS

Announcing a **BRAND-NEW**
multimedia subscription service
for romance fans like you!

Read, Watch and Play.

Experience the easiest way to get
the romance content you crave.

Start your **FREE 7 DAY TRIAL** at
<u>www.harlequinplus.com/freetrial</u>.